The Wanderi1 (Volume 0

Eugène Sue

Alpha Editions

This edition published in 2024

ISBN 9789362993816

Design and Setting By
Alpha Editions
www.alphaedis.com
Email - info@alphaedis.com

As per information held with us this book is in Public Domain.
This book is a reproduction of an important historical work.
Alpha Editions uses the best technology to reproduce historical work
in the same manner it was first published to preserve its original nature.
Any marks or number seen are left intentionally to preserve.

Contents

BOOK VI.	- 1 -
CHAPTER XXVI.	- 2 -
CHAPTER XXVII.	- 11 -
CHAPTER XXVIII.	- 23 -
CHAPTER XXIX.	- 33 -
CHAPTER XXX.	- 39 -
CHAPTER XXXI.	- 45 -
CHAPTER XXXII.	- 53 -
CHAPTER XXXIII.	- 60 -
CHAPTER XXXIV.	- 68 -
CHAPTER XXXV.	- 77 -
CHAPTER XXXVI.	- 86 -
CHAPTER XXXVII.	- 93 -
CHAPTER XXXVIII.	- 102 -
CHAPTER XXXIX.	- 110 -

BOOK VI.

CHAPTER XXVI.

A GOOD GENIUS.

The first of the two, whose arrival had interrupted the answer of the notary, was Faringhea. At sight of this man's forbidding countenance, Samuel approached, and said to him: "Who are you, sir?"

After casting a piercing glance at Rodin, who started but soon recovered his habitual coolness, Faringhea replied to Samuel: "Prince Djalma arrived lately from India, in order to be present here this day, as it was recommended to him by an inscription on a medal, which he wore about his neck."

"He, also!" cried Gabriel, who had been the shipmate of the Indian Prince from the Azores, where the vessel in which he came from Alexandria had been driven into port: "he also one of the heirs! In fact, the prince told me during the voyage that his mother was of French origin. But, doubtless, he thought it right to conceal from me the object of his journey. Oh! that Indian is a noble and courageous young man. Where is he?"

The Strangler again looked at Rodin, and said, laying strong emphasis upon his words: "I left the prince yesterday evening. He informed me that, although he had a great interest to be here, he might possibly sacrifice that interest to other motives. I passed the night in the same hotel, and this morning, when I went to call on him, they told me he was already gone out. My friendship for him led me to come hither, hoping the information I should be able to give might be of use to the prince."

In making no mention of the snare into which he had fallen the day before, in concealing Rodin's machinations with regard to Djalma, and in attributing the absence of this latter to a voluntary cause, the Strangler evidently wished to serve the socius, trusting that Rodin would know how to recompense his discretion. It is useless to observe, that all this story was impudently false. Having succeeded that morning in escaping from his prison by a prodigious effort of cunning, audacity, and skill, he had run to the hotel where he had left Djalma; there he had learned that a man and woman, of an advanced age, and most respectable appearance, calling themselves relations of the young Indian, had asked to see him—and that, alarmed at the dangerous state of somnolency in which he seemed to be plunged, they had taken him home in their carriage, in order to pay him the necessary attention.

"It is unfortunate," said the notary, "that this heir also did not make his appearance—but he has, unhappily, forfeited his right to the immense inheritance that is in question."

"Oh! an immense inheritance is in question," said Faringhea, looking fixedly at Rodin, who prudently turned away his eyes.

The second of the two personages we have mentioned entered at this moment. It was the father of Marshal Simon, an old man of tall stature, still active and vigorous for his age. His hair was white and thin. His countenance, rather fresh-colored, was expressive at once of quickness, mildness and energy.

Agricola advanced hastily to meet him. "You here, M. Simon!" he exclaimed.

"Yes, my boy," said the marshal's father, cordially pressing Agricola's hand "I have just arrived from my journey. M. Hardy was to have been here, about some matter of inheritance, as he supposed: but, as he will still be absent from Paris for some time, he has charged me—"

"He also an heir!—M. Francis Hardy!" cried Agricola, interrupting the old workman.

"But how pale and agitated you are, my boy!" said the marshal's father, looking round with astonishment. "What is the matter?"

"What is the matter?" cried Dagobert, in despair, as he approached the foreman. "The matter is that they would rob your granddaughters, and that I have brought them from the depths of Siberia only to witness this shameful deed!"

"Eh?" cried the old workman, trying to recognize the soldiers face, "you are then—"

"Dagobert."

"You—the generous, devoted friend of my son!" cried the marshal's father, pressing the hands of Dagobert in his own with strong emotion; "but did you not speak of Simon's daughter?"

"Of his daughters; for he is more fortunate than he imagines," said Dagobert. "The poor children are twins."

"And where are they?" asked the old man.

"In a convent."

"In a convent?"

"Yes; by the treachery of this man, who keeps them there in order to disinherit them."

"What man?"

"The Marquis d'Aigrigny."

"My son's mortal enemy!" cried the old workman, as he threw a glance of aversion at Father d'Aigrigny, whose audacity did not fail him.

"And that is not all," added Agricola. "M. Hardy, my worthy and excellent master, has also lost his right to this immense inheritance."

"What?" cried Marshal Simon's father; "but M. Hardy did not know that such important interests were concerned. He set out hastily to join one of his friends who was in want of him."

At each of these successive revelations, Samuel felt his trouble increase: but he could only sigh over it, for the will of the testator was couched, unhappily, in precise and positive terms.

Father d'Aigrigny, impatient to end this scene, which caused him cruel embarrassment, in spite of his apparent calmness, said to the notary, in a grave and expressive voice: "It is necessary, sir, that all this should have an end. If calumny could reach me, I would answer victoriously by the facts that have just come to light. Why attribute to odious conspiracies the absence of the heirs, in whose names this soldier and his son have so uncourteously urged their demands? Why should such absence be less explicable than the young Indian's, or than M. Hardy's, who, as his confidential man has just told us, did not even know the importance of the interests that called him hither? Is it not probable, that the daughters of Marshal Simon, and Mdlle. de Cardoville have been prevented from coming here to-day by some very natural reasons? But, once again, this has lasted too long. I think M. Notary will agree with me, that this discovery of new heirs does not at all affect the question, which I had the honor to propose to him just now; namely whether, as trustee for the poor, to whom Abbe Gabriel made a free gift of all he possessed, I remain notwithstanding his tardy and illegal opposition, the only possessor of this property, which I have promised, and which I now again promise, in presence of all here assembled, to employ for the Greater Glory of the Lord? Please to answer me plainly, M. Notary; and thus terminate the scene which must needs be painful to us all."

"Sir," replied the notary, in a solemn tone, "on my soul and conscience, and in the name of law and justice—as a faithful and impartial executor of the last will of M. Marius de Rennepont, I declare that, by virtue of the deed of gift of Abbe Gabriel de Rennepont, you, M. l'Abbe d'Aigrigny, are the only possessor of this property, which I place at your immediate disposal, that you may employ the same according to the intention of the donor."

These words pronounced with conviction and gravity, destroyed the last vague hopes that the representatives of the heirs might till then have entertained. Samuel became paler than usual, and pressed convulsively the hand of Bathsheba, who had drawn near to him. Large tears rolled down the cheeks of the two old people. Dagobert and Agricola were plunged into the deepest dejection. Struck with the reasoning of the notary, who refused to give more credence and authority to their remonstrances than the magistrates had done before him, they saw themselves forced to abandon every hope. But Gabriel suffered more than any one; he felt the most terrible remorse, in reflecting that, by his blindness, he had been the involuntary cause and instrument of this abominable theft.

So, when the notary, after having examined and verified the amount of securities contained in the cedar box, said to Father d'Aigrigny: "Take possession, sir, of this casket—" Gabriel exclaimed, with bitter disappointment and profound despair: "Alas! one would fancy, under these circumstances, that an inexorable fatality pursues all those who are worthy of interest, affection or respect. Oh, my God!" added the young priest, clasping his hands with fervor, "Thy sovereign justice will never permit the triumph of such iniquity."

It was as if heaven had listened to the prayer of the missionary. Hardly had he spoken, when a strange event took place.

Without waiting for the end of Gabriel's invocation, Rodin, profiting by the decision of the notary, had seized the casket in his arms, unable to repress a deep aspiration of joy and triumph. At the very moment when Father d'Aigrigny and his socius thought themselves at last in safe possession of the treasure, the door of the apartment in which the clock had been heard striking was suddenly opened.

A woman appeared upon the threshold.

At sight of her, Gabriel uttered a loud cry, and remained as if thunderstruck. Samuel and Bathsheba fell on their knees together, and raised their clasped hands. The Jew and Jewess felt inexplicable hopes reviving within them.

All the other actors in this scene appeared struck with stupor. Rodin—Rodin himself—recoiled two steps, and replaced the casket on the table with a trembling hand. Though the incident might appear natural enough—a woman appearing on the threshold of a door, which she had just thrown open—there was a pause of deep and solemn silence. Every bosom seemed oppressed, and as if struggling for breath. All experienced, at sight of this woman, surprise mingled with fear, and indefinable anxiety—for this woman was the living original of the portrait, which had been placed in the room a hundred and fifty years ago. The same head-dress, the same flowing robe, the same countenance, so full of poignant and resigned grief! She advanced slowly, and without appearing to perceive the deep impression she had caused. She approached one of the pieces of furniture, inlaid with brass, touched a spring concealed in the moulding of gilded bronze, so that an upper drawer flew open, and taking from it a sealed parchment envelope, she walked up to the table, and placed this packet before the notary, who, hitherto silent and motionless, received it mechanically from her.

Then, casting upon Gabriel, who seemed fascinated by her presence, a long, mild, melancholy look, this woman directed her steps towards the hall, the door of which had remained open. As she passed near Samuel and Bathsheba, who were still kneeling, she stopped an instant, bowed her fair head towards them, and looked at them with tender solicitude. Then, giving them her hands to kiss, she glided away as slowly as she had entered—throwing a last glance upon Gabriel. The departure of this woman seemed to break the spell under which all present had remained for the last few minutes. Gabriel was the first to speak, exclaiming, in an agitated voice. "It is she—again—here—in this house!"

"Who, brother?" said Agricola, uneasy at the pale and almost wild looks of the missionary; for the smith had not yet remarked the strange resemblance of the woman to the portrait, though he shared in the general feeling of amazement, without being able to explain it to himself. Dagobert and Faringhea were in a similar state of mind.

"Who is this woman?" resumed Agricola, as he took the hand of Gabriel, which felt damp and icy cold.

"Look!" said the young priest. "Those portraits have been there for more than a century and a half."

He pointed to the paintings before which he was now seated, and Agricola, Dagobert, and Faringhea raised their eyes to either side of the fireplace. Three exclamations were now heard at once.

"It is she—it is the same woman!" cried the smith, in amazement, "and her portrait has been here for a hundred and fifty years!"

"What do I see?" cried Dagobert, as he gazed at the portrait of the man. "The friend and emissary of Marshal Simon. Yes! it is the same face that I saw last year in Siberia. Oh, yes! I recognize that wild and sorrowful air—those black eyebrows, which make only one!"

"My eyes do not deceive me," muttered Faringhea to himself, shuddering with horror. "It is the same man, with the black mark on his forehead, that we strangled and buried on the banks of the Ganges—the same man, that one of the sons of Bowanee told me, in the ruins of Tchandi, had been met by him afterwards at one of the gates of Bombay—the man of the fatal curse, who scatters death upon his passage—and his picture has existed for a hundred and fifty years!"

And, like Dagobert and Agricola, the stranger could not withdraw his eyes from that strange portrait.

"What a mysterious resemblance!" thought Father d'Aigrigny. Then, as if struck with a sudden idea, he said to Gabriel: "But this woman is the same that saved your life in America?"

"It is the same," answered Gabriel, with emotion; "and yet she told me she was going towards the North," added the young priest, speaking to himself.

"But how came she in this house?" said Father d'Aigrigny, addressing Samuel. "Answer me! did this woman come in with you, or before you?"

"I came in first, and alone, when this door was first opened since a century and half," said Samuel, gravely.

"Then how can you explain the presence of this woman here?" said Father d'Aigrigny.

"I do not try to explain it," said the Jew. "I see, I believe, and now I hope." added he, looking at Bathsheba with an indefinable expression.

"But you ought to explain the presence of this woman!" said Father d'Aigrigny, with vague uneasiness. "Who is she? How came she hither?"

"All I know is, sir, that my father has often told me; there are subterraneous communications between this house and distant parts of the quarter."

"Oh! then nothing can be clearer," said Father d'Aigrigny; "it only remains to be known what this woman intends by coming hither. As for her singular resemblance to this portrait, it is one of the freaks of nature."

Rodin had shared in the general emotion, at the apparition of this mysterious woman. But when he saw that she had delivered a sealed packet to the notary, the socius, instead of thinking of the strangeness of this unexpected vision, was only occupied with a violent desire to quit the house with the treasure which had just fallen to the Company. He felt a vague anxiety at sight of the envelope with the black seal, which the protectress of Gabriel had delivered to the notary, and was still held mechanically in his hands. The socius, therefore, judging this a very good opportunity to walk off with the casket, during the general silence and stupor which still continued, slightly touched Father d'Aigrigny's elbow, made him a sign of intelligence, and, tucking the cedar-wood chest under his arm, was hastening towards the door.

"One moment, sir," said Samuel, rising, and standing in his path; "I request M. Notary to examine the envelope, that has just been delivered to him. You may then go out."

"But, sir," said Rodin, trying to force a passage, "the question is definitively decided in favor of Father d'Aigrigny. Therefore, with your permission—"

"I tell you, sir," answered the old man, in a loud voice, "that this casket shall not leave the house, until M. Notary has examined the envelope just delivered to him!"

These words drew the attention of all, Rodin was forced to retrace his steps. Notwithstanding the firmness of his character, the Jew shuddered at the look of implacable hate which Rodin turned upon him at this moment.

Yielding to the wish of Samuel, the notary examined the envelope with attention. "Good Heaven!" he cried suddenly; "what do I see?—Ah! so much the better!"

At this exclamation all eyes turned upon the notary. "Oh! read, read, sir!" cried Samuel, clasping his hands together. "My presentiments have not then deceived me!"

"But, sir," said Father d'Aigrigny to the notary, for he began to share in the anxiety of Rodin, "what is this paper?"

"A codicil," answered the notary; "a codicil, which reopens the whole question."

"How, sir?" cried Father d'Aigrigny, in a fury, as he hastily drew nearer to the notary, "reopens the whole question! By what right?"

"It is impossible," added Rodin. "We protest against it."

"Gabriel! father! listen," cried Agricola, "all is not lost. There is yet hope. Do you hear, Gabriel? There is yet hope."

"What do you say?" exclaimed the young priest, rising, and hardly believing the words of his adopted brother.

"Gentlemen," said the notary; "I will read to you the superscription of this envelope. It changes, or rather, it adjourns, the whole of the testamentary provisions."

"Gabriel!" cried Agricola, throwing himself on the neck of the missionary, "all is adjourned, nothing is lost!"

"Listen, gentlemen," said the notary; and he read as follows:

"'This is a Codicil, which for reasons herein stated, adjourns and prorogues to the 1st day of June, 1832, though without any other change, all the provisions contained in the testament made by me, at one o'clock this afternoon. The house shall be reclosed, and the funds left in the hands of the same trustee, to be distributed to the rightful claimants on the 1st of June, 1832.

"'Villetaneuse, this 13th of February, 1682, eleven o'clock at night.
"'MARIUS DE RENNEPONT.'"

"I protest against this codicil as a forgery!" cried Father d'Aigrigny livid with rage and despair.

"The woman who delivered it to the notary is a suspicious character," added Rodin. "The codicil has been forged."

"No, sir," said the notary, severely; "I have just compared the two signatures, and they are absolutely alike. For the rest—what I said this morning, with regard to the absent heirs, is now applicable to you—the law is open; you may dispute the authenticity of this codicil. Meanwhile, everything will remain suspended—since the term for the adjustment of the inheritance is prolonged for three months and a half."

When the notary had uttered these last words, Rodin's nails dripped blood; for the first time, his wan lips became red.

"Oh, God! Thou hast heard and granted my prayer!" cried Gabriel, kneeling down with religious fervor, and turning his angelic face towards heaven. "Thy sovereign justice has not let iniquity triumph!"

"What do you say, my brave boy?" cried Dagobert, who, in the first tumult of joy, had not exactly understood the meaning of the codicil.

"All is put off, father!" exclaimed the smith; "the heirs will have three months and a half more to make their claim. And now that these people are unmasked," added Agricola, pointing to Rodin and Father d'Aigrigny, "we have nothing more to fear from them. We shall be on our guard; and the orphans, Mdlle. de Cardoville, my worthy master, M. Hardy, and this young Indian, will all recover their own."

We must renounce the attempt to paint the delight, the transport of Gabriel and Agricola, of Dagobert, and Marshal Simon's father, of Samuel and Bathsheba. Faringhea alone remained in gloomy silence, before the portrait of the man with the black-barred forehead. As for the fury of Father d'Aigrigny and Rodin, when they saw Samuel retake possession of the casket, we must also renounce any attempt to describe it. On the notary's suggestion, who took with him the codicil, to have it opened according to the formalities of the law, Samuel agreed that it would be more prudent to deposit in the Bank of France the securities of immense value that were now known to be in his possession.

While all the generous hearts, which had for a moment suffered so much, were overflowing with happiness, hope, and joy, Father d'Aigrigny and Rodin quitted the house with rage and death in their souls. The reverend father got into his carriage, and said to his servants: "To Saint-Dizier House!"—Then, worn out and crushed, he fell back upon the seat, and hid his face in his hands, while he uttered a deep groan. Rodin sat next to him, and looked with a mixture of anger and disdain at this so dejected and broken-spirited man.

"The coward!" said he to himself. "He despairs—and yet—"

A quarter of an hour later, the carriage stopped in the Rue de Babylone, in the court-yard of Saint-Dizier House.

CHAPTER XXVII.

THE FIRST LAST, AND THE LAST FIRST.

The carriage had travelled rapidly to Saint-Dizier House. During all the way, Rodin remained mute, contenting himself with observing Father d'Aigrigny, and listening to him, as he poured forth his grief and fury in a long monologue, interrupted by exclamations, lamentations, and bursts of rage, directed against the strokes of that inexorable destiny, which had ruined in a moment the best founded hopes. When the carriage entered the courtyard, and stopped before the portico, the princess's face could be seen through one of the windows, half hidden by the folds of a curtain; in her burning anxiety, she came to see if it was really Father d'Aigrigny who arrived at the house. Still more, in defiance of all ordinary rules, this great lady, generally so scrupulous as to appearances, hurried from her apartment, and descended several steps of the staircase, to meet Father d'Aigrigny, who was coming up with a dejected air. At sight of the livid and agitated countenance of the reverend father, the princess stopped suddenly, and grew pale. She suspected that all was lost. A look rapidly exchanged with her old lover left her no doubt of the issue she so much feared. Rodin humbly followed the reverend father, and both, preceded by the princess, entered the room. The door once closed, the princess, addressing Father d'Aigrigny, exclaimed with unspeakable anguish: "What has happened?"

Instead of answering this question, the reverend father, his eyes sparkling with rage, his lips white, his features contracted, looked fixedly at the princess, and said to her: "Do you know the amount of this inheritance, that we estimated at forty millions?"

"I understand," cried the princess; "we have been deceived. The inheritance amounts to nothing, and all you have dare has been in vain."

"Yes, it has indeed been in vain," answered the reverend father, grinding his teeth with rage; "it was no question of forty millions, but of two hundred and twelve millions.

"Two hundred and twelve millions!" repeated the princess in amazement, as she drew back a step. "It is impossible!"

"I tell you I saw the vouchers, which were examined by the notary."

"Two hundred and twelve millions?" resumed the princess, with deep dejection. "It is an immense and sovereign power—and you have renounced—you have not struggled for it, by every possible means, and till the last moment?"

"Madame, I have done all that I could!—notwithstanding the treachery of Gabriel, who this very morning declared that he renounced us, and separated from the Society."

"Ungrateful!" said the princess, unaffectedly.

"The deed of gift, which I had the precaution to have prepared by the notary, was in such good, legal form, that in spite of the objections of that accursed soldier and his son, the notary had put me in possession of the treasure."

"Two hundred and twelve millions!" repeated the princess clasping her hands. "Verily it is like a dream!"

"Yes," replied Father d'Aigrigny, bitterly, "for us, this possession is indeed a dream, for a codicil has been discovered, which puts off for three months and a half all the testamentary provisions. Now that our very precautions have roused the suspicion of all these heirs—now that they know the enormous amount at stake—they will be upon their guard; and all is lost."

"But who is the wretch that produced this codicil?"

"A woman."

"What woman?"

"Some wandering creature, that Gabriel says he met in America, where she saved his life."

"And how could this woman be there—how could she know the existence of this codicil?"

"I think it was all arranged with a miserable Jew, the guardian of the house, whose family has had charge of the funds for three generations; he had no doubt some secret instructions, in case he suspected the detention of any of the heirs, for this Marius de Rennepont had foreseen that our Company would keep their eyes upon his race."

"But can you not dispute the validity of this codicil?"

"What, go to law in these times—litigate about a will—incur the certainty of a thousand clamors, with no security for success?—It is bad enough, that even this should get wind. Alas! it is terrible. So near the goal! after so much care and trouble. An affair that had been followed up with so much perseverance during a century and a half!"

"Two hundred and twelve millions!" said the princess. "The Order would have had no need to look for establishments in foreign countries; with such resources, it would have been able to impose itself upon France."

"Yes," resumed Father d'Aigrigny, with bitterness; "by means of education, we might have possessed ourselves of the rising generation. The power is altogether incalculable." Then, stamping with his foot, he resumed: "I tell you, that it is enough to drive one mad with rage! an affair so wisely, ably, patiently conducted!"

"Is there no hope?"

"Only that Gabriel may not revoke his donation, in as far as concerns himself. That alone would be a considerable sum—not less than thirty millions."

"It is enormous—it is almost what you hoped," said the princess; "then why despair?"

"Because it is evident that Gabriel will dispute this donation. However legal it may be, he will find means to annul it, now that he is free, informed as to our designs, and surrounded by his adopted family. I tell you, that all is lost. There is no hope left. I think it will be even prudent to write to Rome, to obtain permission to leave Paris for a while. This town is odious to me!"

"Oh, yes! I see that no hope is left—since you, my friend, have decided almost to fly."

Father d'Aigrigny was completely discouraged and broken down; this terrible blow had destroyed all life and energy within him. He threw himself back in an arm-chair, quite overcome. During the preceding dialogue, Rodin was standing humbly near the door, with his old hat in his hand. Two or three times, at certain passages in the conversation between Father d'Aigrigny and the princess, the cadaverous face of the socius, whose wrath appeared to be concentrated, was slightly flushed, and his flappy eyelids were tinged with red, as if the blood mounted in consequence of an interior struggle; but, immediately after, his dull countenance resumed its pallid blue.

"I must write instantly to Rome, to announce this defeat, which has become an event of the first importance, because it overthrows immense hopes," said Father d'Aigrigny, much depressed.

The reverend father had remained seated; pointing to a table, he said to Rodin, with an abrupt and haughty air:

"Write!"

The socius placed his hat on the ground, answered with a respectful bow the command, and with stooping head and slanting walk, went to seat himself on a chair, that stood before a desk. Then, taking pen and paper, he waited, silent and motionless, for the dictation of his superior.

"With your permission, princess?" said Father d'Aigrigny to Madame de Saint-Dizier. The latter answered by an impatient wave of the hand, as if she reproached him for the formal demand at such a time. The reverend father bowed, and dictated these words in a hoarse and hollow voice: "All our hopes, which of late had become almost certainties, have been suddenly defeated. The affair of the Rennepont inheritance, in spite of all the care and skill employed upon it, has completely and finally failed. At the point to which matters had been brought, it is unfortunately worse than a failure; it is a most disastrous event for the Society, which was clearly entitled to this property, fraudulently withdrawn from a confiscation made in our favor. My conscience at least bears witness, that, to the last moment, I did all that was possible to defend and secure our rights. But I repeat, we must consider this important affair as lost absolutely and forever, and think no more about it."

Thus dictating, Father d'Aigrigny's back was turned towards Rodin. At a sudden movement made by the socius, in rising and throwing his pen upon the table, instead of continuing to write, the reverend father turned round, and, looking at Rodin with profound astonishment, said to him: "Well! what are you doing?"

"It is time to end this—the man is mad!" said Rodin to himself, as he advanced slowly towards the fireplace.

"What! you quit your place—you cease writing?" said the reverend father, in amazement. Then, addressing the princess, who shared in his astonishment, he added, as he glanced contemptuously at the socius, "He is losing his senses."

"Forgive him," replied Mme. de Saint-Dizier; "it is, no doubt, the emotion caused by the ruin of this affair."

"Thank the princess, return to your place, and continue to write," said Father d'Aigrigny to Rodin, in a tone of disdainful compassion, as, with imperious finger, he pointed to the table.

The socius, perfectly indifferent to this new order, approached the fireplace, drew himself up to his full height as he turned his arched back, planted himself firmly on his legs, stamped on the carpet with the heel of his clumsy, greasy shoes, crossed his hands beneath the flaps of his old, spotted coat, and, lifting his head, looked fixedly at Father d'Aigrigny. The socius had not spoken a word, but his hideous countenance, now flushed, suddenly revealed such a sense of his superiority, and such sovereign contempt for Father d'Aigrigny, mingled with so calm and serene a daring, that the reverend father and the princess were quite confounded by it. They felt themselves overawed by this little old man, so sordid and so ugly. Father d'Aigrigny knew too well the customs of the Company, to believe his humble secretary capable of assuming so suddenly these airs of transcendent superiority without a motive, or rather, without a positive right. Late, too late, the reverend father perceived, that this subordinate agent might be partly a spy, partly an experienced assistant, who, according to the constitutions of the Order, had the power and mission to depose and provisionally replace, in certain urgent cases, the incapable person over whom he was stationed as a guard. The reverend father was not deceived. From the general to the provincials, and to the rectors of the colleges, all the superior members of the Order have stationed near them, often without their knowledge, and in apparently the lowest capacities, men able to assume their functions at any given moment, and who, with this view, constantly keep up a direct correspondence with Rome.

From the moment Rodin had assumed this position, the manners of Father d'Aigrigny, generally so haughty, underwent a change. Though it cost him a good deal, he said with hesitation, mingled with deference: "You have, no doubt, the right to command me—who hitherto have commanded." Rodin, without answering, drew from his well-rubbed and greasy pocket-book a slip of paper, stamped upon both sides, on which were written several lines in Latin. When he had read it, Father d'Aigrigny pressed this paper respectfully, even religiously, to his lips: then returned it to Rodin, with a low bow. When he again raised his head, he was purple with shame and vexation. Notwithstanding his habits of passive obedience and immutable respect for the will of the Order, he felt a bitter and violent rage at seeing himself thus abruptly deposed from power. That was not all. Though, for a long time past, all relations in gallantry had ceased between him and Mme. de Saint-Dizier, the latter was not the less a woman; and for him to suffer this humiliation in presence of a woman was, undoubtedly, cruel, as, notwithstanding his entrance into the Order, he had not wholly laid aside the character of man of the world. Moreover, the princess, instead of appearing hurt and offended by this sudden transformation of the superior into a subaltern, and of the subaltern into a superior, looked at Rodin with a sort of curiosity mingled with interest. As a woman—as a woman, intensely ambitious, seeking to connect herself with every powerful influence—the princess loved this strange species of contrast. She found it curious and interesting to see this man, almost in rags, mean in appearance, and ignobly ugly, and but lately the most humble of subordinates look down from the height of his superior intelligence upon the nobleman by birth, distinguished for the elegance of his manners, and just before so considerable a personage in the Society. From that moment, as the more important personage of the two, Rodin completely took the place of Father d'Aigrigny in the princess's mind. The first pang of humiliation over, the reverend father, though his pride bled inwardly, applied all his knowledge of the world to behave with redoubled courtesy towards Rodin, who had become his superior by this abrupt change of fortune. But the ex-socius, incapable of appreciating, or rather of acknowledging, such delicate shades of manner, established himself at once, firmly, imperiously, brutally, in his new position, not from any reaction of offended pride, but from a consciousness of what he was really worth. A long acquaintance with Father d'Aigrigny had revealed to him the inferiority of the latter.

"You threw away your pen," said Father d'Aigrigny to Rodin with extreme deference, "while I was dictating a note for Rome. Will you do me the favor to tell me how I have acted wrong?"

"Directly," replied Rodin, in his sharp, cutting voice. "For a long time this affair appeared to me above your strength; but I abstained from interfering. And yet what mistakes! what poverty of invention; what coarseness in the means employed to bring it to bear!"

"I can hardly understand your reproaches," answered Father d'Aigrigny, mildly, though a secret bitterness made its way through his apparent submission. "Was not the success certain, had it not been for this codicil? Did you not yourself assist in the measures that you now blame?"

"You commanded, then, and it was my duty to obey. Besides, you were just on the point of succeeding—not because of the means you had taken—but in spite of those means, with all their awkward and revolting brutality."

"Sir—you are severe," said Father d'Aigrigny.

"I am just. One has to be prodigiously clever, truly, to shut up any one in a room, and then lock the door! And yet, what else have you done? The daughters of General Simon?—imprisoned at Leipsic, shut up in a convent at Paris! Adrienne de Cardoville?—placed in confinement. Sleepinbuff—put in prison. Djalma?—quieted by a narcotic. One only ingenious method, and a thousand times safer, because it acted morally, not materially, was employed to remove M. Hardy. As for your other proceedings—they were all bad, uncertain, dangerous. Why? Because they were violent, and violence provokes violence. Then it is no longer a struggle of keen, skillful, persevering men, seeing through the darkness in which they walk, but a match of fisticuffs in broad day. Though we should be always in action, we should always shrink from view; and yet you could find no better plan than to draw universal attention to us by proceedings at once open and deplorably notorious. To make them more secret, you call in the guard, the commissary of police, the jailers, for your accomplices. It is pitiable, sir; nothing but the most brilliant success could cover such wretched folly; and this success has been wanting."

"Sir," said Father d'Aigrigny, deeply hurt, for the Princess de Saint Dizier, unable to conceal the sort of admiration caused in her by the plain, decisive words of Rodin, looked at her old lover, with an air that seemed to say, "He is right;"—"sir, you are more than severe in your judgment; and, notwithstanding the deference I owe to you, I must observe, that I am not accustomed—"

"There are many other things to which you are not accustomed," said Rodin, harshly interrupting the reverend father; "but you will accustom yourself to them. You have hitherto had a false idea of your own value. There is the old leaven of the soldier and the worlding fermenting within you, which deprives your reason of the coolness, lucidity, and penetration that it ought to possess. You have been a fine military officer, brisk and gay, foremost in wars and festivals, with pleasures and women. These things have half worn you out. You will never be anything but a subaltern; you have been thoroughly tested. You will always want that vigor and concentration of mind which governs men and events. That vigor and concentration of mind I have—and do you know why? It is because, solely devoted to the service of the Company, I have always been ugly, dirty, unloved, unloving—I have all my manhood about me!"

In pronouncing these words, full of cynical pride, Rodin was truly fearful. The princess de Saint-Dizier thought him almost handsome by his energy and audacity.

Father d'Aigrigny, feeling himself overawed, invincibly and inexorably, by this diabolical being, made a last effort to resist and exclaimed, "Oh! sir, these boastings are no proofs of valor and power. We must see you at work."

"Yes," replied Rodin, coldly; "do you know at what work?" Rodin was fond of this interrogative mode of expression. "Why, at the work that you so basely abandon."

"What!" cried the Princess de Saint-Dizier; for Father d'Aigrigny, stupefied at Rodin's audacity, was unable to utter a word.

"I say," resumed Rodin, slowly, "that I undertake to bring to a good issue this affair of the Rennepont inheritance, which appears to you so desperate."

"You?" cried Father d'Aigrigny. "You?"
"I."

"But they have unmasked our maneuvers."

"So much the better; we shall be obliged to invent others."

"But they; will suspect us in everything."

"So much the better; the success that is difficult is the most certain."

"What! do you hope to make Gabriel consent not to revoke his donation, which is perhaps illegal?"

"I mean to bring in to the coffers of the Company the whole of the two hundred and twelve millions, of which they wish to cheat us. Is that clear?"

"It is clear—but impossible."

"And I tell you that it is, and must be possible. Do you not understand, short-sighted as you are!" cried Rodin, animated to such a degree that his cadaverous face became slightly flushed; "do you not understand that it is no longer in our choice to hesitate? Either these two hundred and twelve millions must be ours—and then the re-establishment of our sovereign influence in France is sure—for, in these venal times, with such a sum at command, you may bribe or overthrow a government, or light up the flame of civil war, and restore legitimacy, which is our natural ally, and, owing all to us, would give us all in return—"

"That is clear," cried the princess, clasping her hands in admiration.

"If, on the contrary," resumed Rodin, "these two hundred and twelve millions fall into the hands of the family of the Renneponts, it will be our ruin and our destruction. We shall create a stock of bitter and implacable enemies. Have you not heard the execrable designs of that Rennepont, with regard to the association he recommends, and which, by an accursed fatality, his race are just in a condition to realize? Think of the forces that would rally round these millions. There would be Marshal Simon, acting in the name of his daughters—that is, the man of the people become a duke, without being the vainer for it, which secures his influence with the mob, because military spirit and Bonapartism still represent, in the eyes of the French populace, the traditions of national honor and glory. There would be Francis Hardy, the liberal, independent, enlightened citizen, the type of the great manufacturer, the friend of progress, the benefactor of his workmen. There would be Gabriel—the good priest, as they say!—the apostle of the primitive gospel, the representative of the democracy of the church, of the poor country curate as opposed to the rich bishop, the tiller of the vine as opposed to him who sits in the shade of it; the propagator of all the ideas of fraternity, emancipation, progress—to use their own jargon—and that, not in the name of revolutionary and incendiary politics, but in the name of a religion of charity, love, and peace—to speak as they speak. There, too, would be Adrienne de Cardoville, the type of elegance, grace, and beauty, the priestess of the senses, which she deifies by refining and cultivating them. I need not tell you of her wit and audacity; you know them but too well. No one could be more dangerous to us than this creature, a patrician in blood, a plebeian in heart, a poet in imagination. Then, too, there would be Prince Djalma, chivalrous, bold, ready for adventure, knowing nothing of civilized life, implacable in his hate as in his affection, a terrible instrument for whoever can make use of him. In this detestable family, even such a wretch as Sleepinbuff, who in himself is of no value, raised and purified by the contact of these generous and far from narrow natures (as they call them), might represent the working class, and take a large share in the influence of that association. Now do you not think that if all these people, already exasperated against us, because (as they say) we have wished to rob them, should follow the detestable counsels of this Rennepont—should unite their forces around this immense fortune, which would strengthen them a hundred-fold—do you not think that, if they declare a deadly war against us, they will be the most dangerous enemies that we have ever had? I tell you that the Company has never been in such serious peril; yes, it is now a question of life and death. We must no longer defend ourselves, but lead the attack, so as to annihilate this accursed race of Rennepont, and obtain possession of these millions."

At this picture, drawn by Rodin with a feverish animation, which had only the more influence from its unexpectedness, the princess and Father d'Aigrigny looked at each other in confusion.

"I confess," said the reverend father to Rodin, "I had not considered all the dangerous consequences of this association, recommended by M. de Rennepont. I believe that the heir, from the characters we know them to be possessed of, would wish to realize this Utopia. The peril is great and pressing; what is to be done?"

"What, sir? You have to act upon ignorant, heroic, enthusiastic natures like Djalma's—sensual and eccentric characters like Adrienne de Cardoville's—simple and ingenuous minds like Rose and Blanche Simon's—honest and frank dispositions like Francis Hardy's—angelic and pure souls like Gabriel's—brutal and stupid instincts like Jacques—and can you ask, 'What is to be done?'"

"In truth, I do not understand you," said Father d'Aigrigny.

"I believe it. Your past conduct shows as much," replied Rodin, contemptuously. "You have had recourse to the lowest and most mechanical contrivances, instead of acting upon the noble and generous passions, which, once united, would constitute so formidable a bond; but which, now divided and isolated, are open to every surprise, every seduction, every attack! Do you, at length understand me? Not yet?" added Rodin, shrugging his shoulders. "Answer me—do people die of despair?"

"Yes."

"May not the gratitude of successful love reach the last limits of insane generosity?"

"Yes."

"May there not be such horrible deceptions, that suicide is the only refuge from frightful realities?"

"Yes."

"May not the excess of sensuality lead to the grave by a slow and voluptuous agony?"

"Yes."

"Are there not in life such terrible circumstances that the most worldly, the firmest, the most impious characters, throw themselves blindly, overwhelmed with despair, into the arms of religion, and abandon all earthly greatness for sackcloth, and prayers, and solitude?"

"Yes."

"Are there not a thousand occasions in which the reaction of the passions works the most extraordinary changes, and brings about the most tragic catastrophes in the life of man and woman?"

"No doubt."

"Well, then! why ask me, 'What is to be done?' What would you say, for example, if before three months are over, the most dangerous members of this family of the Renneponts should come to implore, upon their knees, admission to that very Society which they now hold in horror, and from which Gabriel has just separated?"

"Such a conversion is impossible," cried Father d'Aigrigny.

"Impossible? What were you, sir, fifteen years ago?" said Rodin. "An impious and debauched man of the world. And yet you came to us, and your wealth became ours. What! we have conquered princes, kings, popes; we have absorbed and extinguished in our unity magnificent intelligences, which, from afar, shone with too dazzling a light; we have all but governed two worlds; we have perpetuated our Society, full of life, rich and formidable, even to this day, through all the hate, and all the persecutions that have assailed us; and yet we shall not be able to get the better of a single family, which threatens our Company, and has despoiled us of a large fortune? What! we are not skillful enough to obtain this result without having recourse to awkward and dangerous violence? You do not know, then, the immense field that is thrown open by the mutually destructive power of human passions, skillfully combined, opposed, restrained, excited?—particularly," added Rodin, with a strange smile, "when, thanks to a powerful ally, these passions are sure to be redoubled in ardor and energy."

"What ally?" asked Father d'Aigrigny, who, as well as the Princess de Saint-Dizier, felt a sort of admiration mixed with terror.

"Yes," resumed Rodin, without answering the reverend father; "this formidable ally, who comes to our assistance, may bring about the most astonishing transformations—make the coward brave, and the impious credulous, and the gentle ferocious—"

"But this ally!" cried the Princess, oppressed with a vague sense of fear. "This great and formidable ally—who is he?"

"If he comes," resumed Rodin, still impassible, "the youngest and most vigorous, every moment in danger of death, will have no advantage over the sick man at his last gasp."

"But who is this ally?" exclaimed Father d'Aigrigny, more and more alarmed, for as the picture became darker, Rodin's face become more cadaverous.

"This ally, who can decimate a population, may carry away with him in the shroud that he drags at his heels, the whole of an accursed race; but even he must respect the life of that great intangible body, which does not perish with the death of its members—for the spirit of the Society of Jesus is immortal!"

"And this ally?"

"Oh, this ally," resumed Rodin, "who advances with slow steps, and whose terrible coming is announced by mournful presentiments—"

"Is—"

"The Cholera!"

These words, pronounced by Rodin in an abrupt voice, made the Princess and Father d'Aigrigny grow pale and tremble. Rodin's look was gloomy and chilling, like a spectre's. For some moments, the silence of the tomb reigned in the saloon. Rodin was the first to break it. Still impassible, he pointed with imperious gesture to the table, where a few minutes before he had himself been humbly seated, and said in a sharp voice to Father d'Aigrigny, "Write!"

The reverend father started at first with surprise; then, remembering that from a superior he had become an inferior, he rose, bowed lowly to Rodin, as he passed before him, seated himself at the table, took the pen, and said, "I am ready."

Rodin dictated, and the reverend Father wrote as follows: "By the mismanagement of the Reverend Father d'Aigrigny, the affair of the inheritance of the Rennepont family has been seriously compromised. The sum amounts to two hundred and twelve millions. Notwithstanding the check we have received, we believe we may safely promise to prevent these Renneponts from injuring the Society, and to restore the two hundred and twelve millions to their legitimate possessors. We only ask for the most complete and extensive powers."

A quarter of an hour after this scene, Rodin left Saint Dizier House, brushing with his sleeve the old greasy hat, I which he had pulled off to return the salute of the porter by a very low bow.

CHAPTER XXVIII.

THE STRANGER.

The following scene took place on the morrow of the day in which Father d'Aigrigny had been so rudely degraded by Rodin to the subaltern position formerly occupied by the socius.

It is well known that the Rue Clovis is one of the most solitary streets in the Montagne St. Genevieve district. At the epoch of this narrative, the house No. 4, in this street, was composed of one principal building, through which ran a dark passage, leading to a little, gloomy court, at the end of which was a second building, in a singularly miserable and dilapidated condition. On the ground-floor, in front of the house, was a half-subterraneous shop, in which was sold charcoal, fagots, vegetables, and milk. Nine o'clock in the morning had just struck. The mistress of the shop, one Mother Arsene, an old woman of a mild, sickly countenance, clad in a brown stuff dress, with a red bandanna round her head, was mounted on the top step of the stairs which led down to her door, and was employed in setting out her goods—that is, on one side of her door she placed a tin milk-can, and on the other some bunches of stale vegetables, flanked with yellowed cabbages. At the bottom of the steps, in the shadowy depths of the cellar, one could see the light of the burning charcoal in a little stove. This shop situated at the side of the passage, served as a porter's lodge, and the old woman acted as portress. On a sudden, a pretty little creature, coming from the house, entered lightly and merrily the shop. This young girl was Rose-Pompon, the intimate friend of the Bacchanal Queen.—Rose-Pompon, a widow for the moment, whose bacchanalian cicisbeo was Ninny Moulin, the orthodox scapegrace, who, on occasion, after drinking his fill, could transform himself into Jacques Dumoulin, the religious writer, and pass gayly from dishevelled dances to ultramontane polemics, from Storm-blown Tulips to Catholic pamphlets.

Rose-Pompon had just quitted her bed, as appeared by the negligence of her strange morning costume; no doubt, for want of any other head-dress, on her beautiful light hair, smooth and well-combed, was stuck jauntily a foraging-cap, borrowed from her masquerading costume. Nothing could be more sprightly than that face, seventeen years old, rosy, fresh, dimpled, and brilliantly lighted up by a pair of gay, sparkling blue eyes. Rose Pompon was so closely enveloped from the neck to the feet in a red and green plaid cloak, rather faded, that one could guess the cause of her modest embarrassment. Her naked feet, so white that one could not tell if she wore stockings or not, were slipped into little morocco shoes, with plated buckles. It was easy to perceive that her cloak concealed some article which she held in her hand.

"Good-day, Rose-Pompon," said Mother Arsene with a kindly air; "you are early this morning. Had you no dance last night?"

"Don't talk of it, Mother Arsene; I had no heart to dance. Poor Cephyse—the Bacchanal Queen—has done nothing but cry all night. She cannot console herself, that her lover should be in prison."

"Now, look here, my girl," said the old woman, "I must speak to you about your friend Cephyse. You won't be angry?"

"Am I ever angry?" said Rose-Pompon, shrugging her shoulders.

"Don't you think that M. Philemon will scold me on his return?"

"Scold you! what for?"

"Because of his rooms, that you occupy."

"Why, Mother Arsene, did not Philemon tell you, that, in his absence, I was to be as much mistress of his two rooms as I am of himself?"

"I do not speak of you, but of your friend Cephyse, whom you have also brought to occupy M. Philemon's lodgings."

"And where would she have gone without me, my good Mother Arsene? Since her lover was arrested, she has not dared to return home, because she owes ever so many quarters. Seeing her troubles. I said to her: 'Come, lodge at Philemon's. When he returns, we must find another place for you.'"

"Well, little lovey—if you only assure me that M. Philemon will not be angry—"

"Angry! for what? That we spoil his things? A fine set of things he has to spoil! I broke his last cup yesterday—and am forced to fetch the milk in this comic concern."

So saying, laughing with all her might, Rose-Pompon drew her pretty little white arm from under her cloak, and presented to Mother Arsene one of those champagne glasses of colossal capacity, which hold about a bottle.

"Oh, dear!" said the greengrocer in amazement; "it is like a glass trumpet."

"It is Philemon's grand gala-glass, which they gave him when he took his degrees in boating," said Rose-Pompon, gravely.

"And to think you must put your milk in it—I am really ashamed," said Mother Arsene.

"So am I! If I were to meet any one on the stairs, holding this glass in my hand like a Roman candlestick, I should burst out laughing, and break the last remnant of Philemon's bazaar, and he would give me his malediction."

"There is no danger that you will meet any one. The first-floor is gone out, and the second gets up very late."

"Talking of lodgers," said Rose-Pompon, "is there not a room to let on the second-floor in the rear house? It might do for Cephyse, when Philemon comes back."

"Yes, there is a little closet in the roof—just over the two rooms of the mysterious old fellow," said Mother Arsene.

"Oh, yes! Father Charlemagne. Have you found out anything more about him?"

"Dear me, no, my girl! only that he came this morning at break of day, and knocked at my shutters. 'Have you received a letter for me, my good lady?' said he—for he is always so polite, the dear man!—'No, sir,' said I.—'Well, then, pray don't disturb yourself, my good lady!' said he; 'I will call again.' And so he went away."

"Does he never sleep in the house?"

"Never. No doubt, he lodges somewhere else—but he passes some hours here, once every four or five days."

"And always comes alone?"

"Always."

"Are you quite sure? Does he never manage to slip in some little puss of a woman? Take care, or Philemon will give you notice to quit," said Rose-Pompon, with an air of mock-modesty.

"M. Charlemagne with a woman! Oh, poor dear man!" said the greengrocer, raising her hands to heaven; "if you saw him, with his greasy hat, his old gray coat, his patched umbrella, and his simple face, he looks more like a saint than anything else."

"But then, Mother Arsene, what does the saint do here, all alone for hours, in that hole at the bottom of the court, where one can hardly see at noon-day?"

"That's what I ask myself, my dovey, what can he be doing? It can't be that he comes to look at his furniture, for he has nothing but a flock bed, a table, a stove, a chair, and an old trunk."

"Somewhat in the style of Philemon's establishment," said Rose-Pompon.

"Well, notwithstanding that, Rosey, he is as much afraid that any one should come into his room, as if we were all thieves, and his furniture was made of massy gold. He has had a patent lock put on the door, at his own expense; he never leaves me his key; and he lights his fire himself, rather than let anybody into his room."

"And you say he is old?"

"Yes, fifty or sixty."

"And ugly?"

"Just fancy, little viper's eyes, looking as if they had been bored with a gimlet, in a face as pale as death—so pale, that the lips are white. That's for his appearance. As for his character, the good old man's so polite!—he pulls off his hat so often, and makes you such low bows, that it is quite embarrassing."

"But, to come back to the point," resumed Rose-Pompon, "what can he do all alone in those two rooms? If Cephyse should take the closet, on Philemon's return, we may amuse ourselves by finding out something about it. How much do they want for the little room?"

"Why, it is in such bad condition, that I think the landlord would let it go for fifty or fifty-five francs a-year, for there is no room for a stove, and the only light comes through a small pane in the roof."

"Poor Cephyse!" said Rose, sighing, and shaking her head sorrowfully. "After having amused herself so well, and flung away so much money with Jacques Rennepont, to live in such a place, and support herself by hard work! She must have courage!"

"Why, indeed, there is a great difference between that closet and the coach-and-four in which Cephyse came to fetch you the other day, with all the fine masks, that looked so gay—particularly the fat man in the silver paper helmet, with the plume and the top boots. What a jolly fellow!"

"Yes, Ninny Moulin. There is no one like him to dance the forbidden fruit. You should see him with Cephyse, the Bacchanal Queen. Poor laughing, noisy thing!—the only noise she makes now is crying."

"Oh! these young people—these young people!" said the greengrocer.

"Easy, Mother Arsene; you were young once."

"I hardly know. I have always thought myself much the same as I am now."

"And your lovers, Mother Arsene?"

"Lovers! Oh, yes! I was too ugly for that—and too well taken care of."

"Your mother looked after you, then?"

"No, my girl; but I was harnessed."

"Harnessed!" cried Rose-Pompon, in amazement, interrupting the dealer.

"Yes,—harnessed to a water-cart, along with my brother. So, you see, when we had drawn like a pair of horses for eight or ten hours a day, I had no heart to think of nonsense."

"Poor Mother Arsene, what a hard life," said Rose-Pompon with interest.

"In the winter, when it froze, it was hard enough. I and my brother were obliged to be rough-shod, for fear of slipping."

"What a trade for a woman! It breaks one's heart. And they forbid people to harness dogs!" added Rose-Pompon, sententiously.[21]

"Why, 'tis true," resumed Mother Arsene. "Animals are sometimes better off than people. But what would you have? One must live, you know. As you make your bed, you must lie. It was hard enough, and I got a disease of the lungs by it—which was not my fault. The strap, with which I was harnessed, pressed so hard against my chest, that I could scarcely breathe: so I left the trade, and took to a shop, which is just to tell you, that if I had had a pretty face and opportunity, I might have done like so many other young people, who begin with laughter and finish—"

"With a laugh t'other side of the mouth—you would say; it is true, Mother Arsene. But, you see, every one has not the courage to go into harness, in order to remain virtuous. A body says to herself, you must have some amusement while you are young and pretty—you will not always be seventeen years old—and then—and then—the world will end, or you will get married."

"But, perhaps, it would have been better to begin by that."

"Yes, but one is too stupid; one does not know how to catch the men, or to frighten them. One is simple, confiding, and they only laugh at us. Why, Mother Arsene, I am myself an example that would make you shudder; but 'tis quite enough to have had one's sorrows, without fretting one's self at the remembrance."

"What, my beauty! you, so young and gay, have had sorrows?"

"Ah, Mother Arsene! I believe you. At fifteen and a half I began to cry, and never left off till I was sixteen. That was enough, I think."

"They deceived you, mademoiselle?"

"They did worse. They treated me as they have treated many a poor girl, who had no more wish to go wrong than I had. My story is not a three volume one. My father and mother are peasants near Saint-Valery, but so poor—so poor, that having five children to provide for, they were obliged to send me, at eight years old, to my aunt, who was a charwoman here in Paris. The good woman took me out of charity, and very kind it was of her, for I earned but little. At eleven years of age she sent me to work in one of the factories of the Faubourg Saint-Antoine. I don't wish to speak, ill of the masters of these factories; but what do they care, if little boys and girls are mixed up pell-mell with young men and women of eighteen to twenty? Now you see, there, as everywhere, some are no better than they should be; they are not particular in word or deed, and I ask you, what art example for the children, who hear and see more than you think for. Then, what happens? They get accustomed as they grow older, to hear and see things, that afterwards will not shock them at all."

"What you say there is true, Rose-Pompon. Poor children! who takes any trouble about them?—not their father or mother, for they are at their daily work."

"Yes, yes, Mother Arsene, it is all very well; it is easy to cry down a young girl that has gone wrong; but if they knew all the ins and outs, they would perhaps pity rather than blame her. To come back to myself—at fifteen years old I was tolerably pretty. One day I had something to ask of the head clerk. I went to him in his private room. He told me he would grant what I wanted, and even take me under his patronage, if I would listen to him; and he began by trying to kiss me. I resisted. Then he said to me:—'You refuse my offer? You shall have no more work; I discharge you from the factory.'"

"Oh, the wicked man!" said Mother Arsene.

"I went home all in tears, and my poor aunt encouraged me not to yield, and she would try to place me elsewhere. Yes—but it was impossible; the factories were all full. Misfortunes never come single; my aunt fell ill, and there was not a sou in the house; I plucked up my courage, and returned to entreat the mercy of the clerk at the factory. Nothing would do. 'So much the worse,' said he; 'you are throwing away your luck. If you had been more complying, I should perhaps have married you.' What could I do, Mother Arsene?—misery was staring me in the face; I had no work; my aunt was ill; the clerk said he would marry me—I did like so many others."

"And when, afterwards, you spoke to him about marriage?"

"Of course he laughed at me, and in six months left me. Then I wept all the tears in my body, till none remained—then I was very ill—and then—I console myself, as one may console one's self for anything. After some changes, I met with Philemon. It is upon him that I revenge myself for what others have done to me. I am his tyrant," added Rose-Pompon, with a tragic air, as the cloud passed away which had darkened her pretty face during her recital to Mother Arsene.

"It is true," said the latter thoughtfully. "They deceive a poor girl—who is there to protect or defend her? Oh! the evil we do does not always come from ourselves, and then—"

"I spy Ninny Moulin!" cried Rose-Pompon, interrupting the greengrocer, and pointing to the other side of the street. "How early abroad! What can he want with me?" and Rose wrapped herself still more closely and modestly in her cloak.

It was indeed Jacques Dumoulin, who advanced with his hat stuck on one side, with rubicund nose and sparkling eye, dressed in a loose coat, which displayed the rotundity of his abdomen. His hands, one of which held a huge cane shouldered like a musket, were plunged into the vast pockets of his outer garment.

Just as he reached the threshold of the door, no doubt with the intention of speaking to the portress, he perceived Rose-Pompon. "What!" he exclaimed, "my pupil already stirring? That is fortunate. I came on purpose to bless her at the rise of morn!"

So saying, Ninny Moulin advanced with open arms towards Rose-Pompon who drew back a step.

"What, ungrateful child!" resumed the writer on divinity. "Will you refuse me the morning's paternal kiss?"

"I accept paternal kisses from none but Philemon. I had a letter from him yesterday, with a jar of preserves, two geese, a bottle of home-made brandy, and an eel. What ridiculous presents! I kept the drink, and changed the rest for two darling live pigeons, which I have installed in Philemon's cabinet, and a very pretty dove-cote it makes me. For the rest, my husband is coming back with seven hundred francs, which he got from his respectable family, under pretence of learning the bass viol, the cornet-a-piston, and the speaking trumpet, so as to make his way in society, and a slap-up marriage—to use your expression—my good child."

"Well, my dear pupil, we will taste the family brandy, and enjoy ourselves in expectation of Philemon and his seven hundred francs."

So saying, Ninny Moulin slapped the pockets of his waistcoat, which gave forth a metallic sound, and added: "I come to propose to you to embellish my life, to-day and to-morrow, and even the day after, if your heart is willing."

"If the announcements are decent and fraternal, my heart does not say no."

"Be satisfied; I will act by you as your grandfather, your great grandfather, your family portrait. We will have a ride, a dinner, the play, a fancy dress ball, and a supper afterwards. Will that suit you?"

"On condition that poor Cephyse is to go with us. It will raise her spirits."

"Well, Cephyse shall be of the party."

"Have you come into a fortune, great apostle?"

"Better than that, most rosy and pompous of all Rose-Pom, pons! I am head editor of a religious journal; and as I must make some appearance in so respectable a concern, I ask every month for four weeks in advance, and three days of liberty. On this condition, I consent to play the saint for twenty-seven days out of thirty, and to be always as grave and heavy as the paper itself."

"A journal! that will be something droll, and dance forbidden steps all alone on the tables of the cafes."

"Yes, it will be droll enough; but not for everybody. They are rich sacristans, who pay the expenses. They don't look to money, provided the journal bites, tears, burns, pounds, exterminates and destroys. On my word of honor, I shall never have been in such a fury!" added Ninny Moulin, with a loud, hoarse laugh. "I shall wash the wounds of my adversaries with venom of the finest vintage, and gall of the first quality."

For his peroration, Ninny Moulin imitated the pop of uncorking a bottle of champagne—which made Rose-Pompon laugh heartily.

"And what," resumed she, "will be the name of your journal of sacristans?"

"It will be called 'Neighborly Love.'"

"Come! that is a very pretty name."

"Wait a little! there is a second title."

"Let us hear it."

"'Neighborly Love; or, the Exterminator of the Incredulous, the Indifferent, the Lukewarm, and Others,' with this motto from the great Bossuet: 'Those who are not for us are against us.'"

"That is what Philemon says in the battles at the Chaumiere, when he shakes his cane."

"Which proves, that the genius of the Eagle of Meaux is universal. I only reproach him for having been jealous of Moliere."

"Bah! actor's jealousy," said Rose-Pompon.

"Naughty girl!" cried Ninny Moulin, threatening her with his finger.

"But if you are going to exterminate Madame de la Sainte-Colombo, who is somewhat lukewarm—how about your marriage?"

"My journal will advance it, on the contrary. Only think! editor-In chief is a superb position; the sacristans will praise, and push, and support, and bless me; I shall get La-Sainte-Colombe—and then, what a life I'll lead!"

At this moment, a postman entered the shop, and delivered a letter to the greengrocer, saying: "For M. Charlemagne, post-paid!"

"My!" said Rose-Pompon; "it is for the little mysterious old man, who has such extraordinary ways. Does it come from far?"

"I believe you; it comes from Italy, from Rome," said Ninny Moulin, looking in his turn at the letter, which the greengrocer held in her hand. "Who is the astonishing little old man of whom you speak?"

"Just imagine to yourself, my great apostle," said Rose-Pompon, "a little old man, who has two rooms at the bottom of that court. He never sleeps there, but comes from time to time, and shuts himself up for hours, without ever allowing any one to enter his lodging, and without any one knowing what he does there."

"He is a conspirator," said Ninny Moulin, laughing, "or else a comer."

"Poor dear man," said Mother Arsene, "what has he done with his false money? He pays me always in sous for the bit of bread and the radish I furnish him for his breakfast."

"And what is the name of this mysterious chap?" asked Dumoulin.

"M. Charlemagne," said the greengrocer. "But look, surely one speaks of the devil, one is sure to see his horns."

"Where's the horns?"

"There, by the side of the house—that little old man, who walks with his neck awry, and his umbrella under his arm."

"M. Rodin!" ejaculated Ninny Moulin, retreating hastily, and descending three steps into the shop, in order not to be seen. Then he added. "You say, that this gentleman calls himself—"

"M. Charlemagne—do you know him?" asked the greengrocer.

"What the devil does he do here, under a false name?" said Jacques Dumoulin to himself.

"You know him?" said Rose-Pompon, with impatience. "You are quite confused."

"And this gentleman has two rooms in this house, and comes here mysteriously," said Jacques Dumoulin, more and more surprised.

"Yes," resumed Rose-Pompon; "you can see his windows from Philemon's dove-cote."

"Quick! quick! let me go into the passage, that I may not meet him," said Dumoulin.

And, without having been perceived by Rodin, he glided from the shop into the passage, and thence mounted to the stairs, which led to the apartment occupied by Rose-Pompon.

"Good-morning, M. Charlemagne," said Mother Arsene to Rodin, who made his appearance on the threshold. "You come twice in a day; that is right, for your visits are extremely rare."

"You are too polite, my good lady," said Rodin, with a very courteous bow; and he entered the shop of the greengrocer.

[21] There are, really, ordinances, full of a touching interest for the canine race, which forbid the harnessing of dogs.

CHAPTER XXIX.

THE DEN.

Rodin's countenance, when he entered Mother Arsene's shop, was expressive of the most simple candor. He leaned his hands on the knob of his umbrella, and said: "I much regret, my good lady, that I roused you so early this morning."

"You do not come often enough, my dear sir, for me to find fault with you."

"How can I help it, my good lady? I live in the country, and only come hither from time to time to settle my little affairs."

"Talking of that sir, the letter you expected yesterday has arrived this morning. It is large, and comes from far. Here it is," said the greengrocer, drawing it from her pocket; "it cost nothing for postage."

"Thank you, my dear lady," said Rodin, taking the letter with apparent indifference, and putting it into the side-pocket of his great-coat, which he carefully buttoned over.

"Are you going up to your rooms, sir?"

"Yes, my good, lady."

"Then I will get ready your little provisions," said Mother Arsene; "as usual, I suppose, my dear sir?"

"Just as usual."

"It shall be ready in the twinkling of an eye, sir."

So saying, the greengrocer took down an old basket; after throwing into it three or four pieces of turf, a little bundle of wood, and some charcoal, she covered all this fuel with a cabbage leaf; then, going to the further end of the shop, she took from a chest a large round loaf, cut off a slice, and selecting a magnificent radish with the eye of a connoisseur, divided it in two, made a hole in it, which she filled with gray salt joined the two pieces together again, and placed it carefully by the side of the bread, on the cabbage leaf which separated the eatables from the combustibles. Finally, taking some embers from the stove, she put them into a little earthen pot, containing ashes, which she placed also in the basket.

Then, reascending to her top step, Mother Arsene said to Rodin: "Here is your basket, sir."

"A thousand thanks, my good lady," answered Rodin, and plunging his hand into the pocket of his trousers, he drew forth eight sous, which he counted out only one by one to the greengrocer, and said to her, as he carried off his store: "Presently, when I come down again, I will return your basket as usual."

"Quite at your service, my dear sir, quite at your service," said Mother Arsene.

Rodin tucked his umbrella under his left arm, took up the greengrocer's basket with his right hand, entered the dark passage, crossed the little court and mounted with light step to the second story of a dilapidated building; there, drawing a key from his pocket, he opened a door, which he locked carefully after him. The first of the two rooms which he occupied was completely unfurnished, as for the second, it is impossible to imagine a more gloomy and miserable den. Papering so much worn, torn and faded, that no one could recognize its primitive color, bedecked the walls. A wretched flock-bed, covered with a moth-fretted blanket; a stool, and a little table of worm-eaten wood; an earthenware stove, as cracked as old china; a trunk with a padlock, placed under the bed—such was the furniture of this desolate hole. A narrow window, with dirty panes, hardly gave any light to this room, which was almost deprived of air by the height of the building in front; two old cotton pocket handkerchiefs, fastened together with pins, and made to slide upon a string stretched across the window, served for curtains. The plaster of the roof, coming through the broken and disjointed tiles, showed the extreme neglect of the inhabitant of this abode. After locking his door, Rodin threw his hat and umbrella on the bed, placed his basket on the ground, set the radish and bread on the table, and kneeling down before his stove, stuffed it with fuel, and lighted it by blowing with vigorous lungs on the embers contained in his earthen pot.

When, to use the consecrated expression, the stove began to draw, Rodin spread out the handkerchiefs, which served him for curtains; then, thinking himself quite safe from every eye, he took from the side-pocket of his great-coat the letter that Mother Arsene had given him. In doing so, he brought out several papers and different articles; one of these papers, folded into a thick and rumpled packet, fell upon the table, and flew open. It contained a silver cross of the Legion of Honor, black with time. The red ribbon of this cross had almost entirely lost its original color. At sight of this cross, which he replaced in his pocket with the medal of which Faringhea had despoiled Djalma, Rodin shrugged his shoulders with a contemptuous and sardonic air; then, producing his large silver watch, he laid it on the table by the side of the letter from Rome. He looked at this letter with a singular mixture of suspicion and hope, of fear, and impatient curiosity. After a moment's reflection, he prepared to unseal the envelope;

but suddenly he threw it down again upon the table, as if, by a strange caprice, he had wished to prolong for a few minutes that agony of uncertainty, as poignant and irritating as the emotion of the gambler.

Looking at his watch, Rodin resolved not to open the letter, until the hand should mark half-past nine, of which it still wanted seven minutes. In one of those whims of puerile fatalism, from which great minds have not been exempt, Rodin said to himself: "I burn with impatience to open this letter. If I do not open it till half-past nine, the news will be favorable." To employ these minutes, Rodin took several turns up and down the room, and stood in admiring contemplation before two old prints, stained with damp and age, and fastened to the wall by rusty nails. The first of these works of art—the only ornaments with which Rodin had decorated this hole—was one of those coarse pictures, illuminated with red, yellow, green, and blue, such as are sold at fairs; an Italian inscription announced that this print had been manufactured at Rome. It represented a woman covered with rags, bearing a wallet, and having a little child upon her knees; a horrible hag of a fortune-teller held in her hands the hand of the little child, and seemed to read there his future fate, for these words in large blue letters issued from her mouth: "Sara Papa" (he shall be Pope).

The second of these works of art, which appeared to inspire Rodin with deep meditations, was an excellent etching, whose careful finish and bold, correct drawing, contrasted singularly with the coarse coloring of the other picture. This rare and splendid engraving, which had cost Rodin six louis (an enormous expense for him), represented a young boy dressed in rags. The ugliness of his features was compensated by the intellectual expression of his strongly marked countenance. Seated on a stone, surrounded by a herd of swine, that he seemed employed in keeping, he was seen in front, with his elbow resting on his knee, and his chin in the palm of his hand. The pensive and reflective attitude of this young man, dressed as a beggar, the power expressed in his large forehead, the acuteness of his penetrating glance, and the firm lines of the mouth, seemed to reveal indomitable resolution, combined with superior intelligence and ready craft. Beneath this figure, the emblems of the papacy encircled a medallion, in the centre of which was the head of an old man, the lines of which, strongly marked, recalled in a striking manner, notwithstanding their look of advanced age, the features of the young swineherd. This engraving was entitled THE YOUTH of SIXTUS V.; the color print was entitled The Prediction.[22]

In contemplating these prints more and more nearly, with ardent and inquiring eye, as though he had asked for hopes or inspirations from them, Rodin had come so close that, still standing, with his right arm bent behind his head, he rested, as it were, against the wall, whilst, hiding his left hand in the pocket of his black trousers, he thus held back one of the flaps of his olive great-coat. For some minutes, he remained in this meditative attitude.

Rodin, as we have said, came seldom to this lodging; according to the rules of his Order, he had till now lived with Father d'Aigrigny, whom he was specially charged to watch. No member of the Society, particularly in the subaltern position which Rodin had hitherto held, could either shut himself in, or possess an article of furniture made to lock. By this means nothing interferes with the mutual spy-system, incessantly carried on, which forms one of the most powerful resources of the Company of Jesus. It was on account of certain combinations, purely personal to himself, though connected on some points with the interests of the Order, that Rodin, unknown to all, had taken these rooms in the Rue Clovis. And it was from the depths of this obscure den that the socius corresponded directly with the most eminent and influential personages of the sacred college. On one occasion, when Rodin wrote to Rome, that Father d'Aigrigny, having received orders to quit France without seeing his dying mother, had hesitated to set out, the socius had added, in form of postscriptum, at the bottom of the letter denouncing to the General of the Order the hesitation of Father d'Aigrigny:

"Tell the Prince Cardinal that he may rely upon me, but I hope for his active aid in return."

This familiar manner of corresponding with the most powerful dignitary of the Order, the almost patronizing tone of the recommendation that Rodin addressed to the Prince Cardinal, proved that the socius, notwithstanding his apparently subaltern position, was looked upon, at that epoch, as a very important personage, by many of the Princes of the Church, who wrote to him at Paris under a false name, making use of a cipher and other customary precautions. After some moments passed in contemplation, before the portrait of Sixtus V., Rodin returned slowly to the table, on which lay the letter, which, by a sort of superstitious delay, he had deferred opening, notwithstanding his extreme curiosity. As it still wanted some minutes of half-past nine, Rodin, in order not to lose time, set about making preparations for his frugal breakfast. He placed on the table, by the side of an inkstand, furnished with pens, the slice of bread and the radish; then seating himself on his stool, with the stove, as it were, between his legs, he drew a horn-handled knife from his pocket, and cutting alternately a morsel of bread and a morsel of radish, with a sharp, well-worn blade, he began his temperate repast with a vigorous appetite, keeping his eye fixed on the hand of his watch. When it reached the momentous hour, he unsealed the envelope with a trembling hand.

It contained two letters. The first appeared to give him little satisfaction; for, after some minutes, he shrugged his shoulders, struck the table impatiently with the handle of his knife, disdainfully pushed aside the letter with the back of his dirty hand, and perused the second epistle, holding his bread in one hand, and with the other mechanically dipping a slice of radish into the gray salt spilt on a corner of the table. Suddenly, Rodin's hand remained motionless. As he progressed in his reading, he appeared more and more interested, surprised, and struck. Rising abruptly, he ran to the window, as if to assure himself, by a second examination of the cipher, that he was not deceived. The news announced to him in the letter seemed to be unexpected. No doubt, Rodin found that he had deciphered correctly, for, letting fall his arms, not in dejection, but with the stupor of a satisfaction as unforeseen as extraordinary, he remained for some time with his head down, and his eyes fixed—the only mark of joy that he gave being manifested by a loud, frequent, and prolonged respiration. Men who are as audacious in their ambition, as they are patient and obstinate in their mining and countermining, are surprised at their own success, when this latter precedes and surpasses their wise and prudent expectations. Rodin was now in this case. Thanks to prodigies of craft, address, and dissimulation, thanks to mighty promises of corruption, thanks to the singular mixture of admiration, fear, and confidence, with which his genius inspired many influential persons, Rodin now learned from members of the pontifical government, that, in case of a possible and probable occurrence, he might, within a given time, aspire, with a good chance of success, to a position which has too often excited the fear, the hate, or the envy of many sovereigns, and which has in turn, been occupied by great, good men, by abominable scoundrels, and by persons risen from the lowest grades of society. But for Rodin to attain this end with certainty, it was absolutely necessary for him to succeed in that project, which he had undertaken to accomplish without violence, and only by the play and the rebound of passions skillfully managed. The project was: To secure for the Society of Jesus the fortune of the Rennepont family.

This possession would thus have a double and immense result; for Rodin, acting in accordance with his personal views, intended to make of his Order (whose chief was at his discretion) a stepping-stone and a means of intimidation. When his first impression of surprise had passed away—an impression that was only a sort of modesty of ambition and self diffidence, not uncommon with men of really superior powers—Rodin looked more coldly and logically on the matter, and almost reproached himself for his surprise. But soon after, by a singular contradiction, yielding to one of those puerile and absurd ideas, by which men are often carried away when they think themselves alone and unobserved, Rodin rose abruptly, took the letter which had caused him such glad surprise, and went to display it, as it were, before the eyes of the young swineherd in the picture: then, shaking his head proudly and triumphantly, casting his reptile-glance on the portrait, he muttered between his teeth, as he placed his dirty finger on the pontifical emblem: "Eh, brother? and I also—perhaps!"

After this ridiculous interpolation, Rodin returned to his seat, and, as if the happy news he had just received had increased his appetite, he placed the letter before him, to read it once more, whilst he exercised his teeth, with a sort of joyous fury, on his hard bread and radish, chanting an old Litany.

There was something strange, great, and, above all, frightful, in the contrast afforded by this immense ambition, already almost justified by events, and contained, as it were, in so miserable an abode. Father d'Aigrigny (who, if not a very superior man, had at least some real value, was a person of high birth, very haughty, and placed in the best society) would never have ventured to aspire to what Rodin thus looked to from the first. The only aim of Father d'Aigrigny, and even this he thought presumptuous, was to be one day elected General of his Order—that Order which embraced the world. The difference of the ambitious aptitudes of these two personages is conceivable. When a man of eminent abilities, of a healthy and vivacious nature, concentrates all the strength of his mind and body upon a single point, remaining, like Rodin, obstinately chaste and frugal, and renouncing every gratification of the heart and the senses—the man, who revolts against the sacred designs of his Creator, does so almost always in favor of some monstrous and devouring passion—some infernal divinity, which, by a sacrilegious pact, asks of him, in return for the bestowal of formidable power, the destruction of every noble sentiment, and of all those ineffable attractions and tender instincts with which the Maker, in His eternal wisdom and inexhaustible munificence, has so paternally endowed His creatures.

During the scene that we have just described, Rodin had not perceived that the curtain of a window on the third story of the building opposite had been partially drawn aside, and had half-revealed the sprightly face of Rose-Pompon, and the Silenus-like countenance of Ninny Moulin. It ensued that Rodin, notwithstanding his barricade of cotton handkerchiefs, had not been completely sheltered from the indiscreet and curious examination of the two dancers of the Storm-blown Tulip.

[22] According to the tradition, it was predicted to the mother of Sixtus V., that he would be pope; and, in his youth, he is said to have kept swine.

CHAPTER XXX.

AN UNEXPECTED VISIT.

Though Rodin had experienced much surprise on reading the second letter from Rome, he did not choose that his answer should betray any such amazement. Having finished his frugal breakfast, he took a sheet of paper, and rapidly wrote in cipher the following note, in the short, abrupt style that was natural to him when not obliged to restrain himself:

"The information does not surprise me. I had foreseen it all. Indecision and cowardice always bear such fruit. This is not enough. Heretical Russia murders Catholic Poland. Rome blesses the murderers, and curses the victims.[23]

"Let it pass.

"In return, Russia guarantees to Rome, by Austria, the bloody suppression of the patriots of Romagna.

"That, too, is well.

"The cut-throat band of good Cardinal Albani is not sufficient for the massacre of the impious liberals. They are weary of the task.

"Not so well. They must go on."

When Rodin had written these last words, his attention was suddenly attracted by the clear and sonorous voice of Rose-Pompon, who, knowing her Beranger by heart, had opened Philemon's window, and, seated on the sill, sang with much grace and prettiness this verse of the immortal song-writer:

> "How wrong you are! Is't you dare say
> That heaven ever scowls on earth?
> The earth that laughs up to its blue,
> The earth that owes it joy and birth?
> Oh, may the wine from vines it warms,
> May holy love thence fluttering down,
> Lend my philosophy their charms,
> To drive away care's direful frown!
> So, firm let's stand,
> Full glass in hand,
> And all evoke
> The God of honest folk!"

This song, in its divine gentleness, contrasted so strangely with the cold cruelty of the few lines written by Rodin, that he started and bit his lips with rage, as he recognized the words of the great poet, truly Christian, who had dealt such rude blows to the false Church. Rodin waited for some moments with angry impatience, thinking the voice would continue; but Rose-Pompon was silent, or only continued to hum, and soon changed to another air, that of the Good Pope, which she entoned, but without words. Rodin, not venturing to look out of his window to see who was this troublesome warbler, shrugged his shoulders, resumed his pen, and continued:

"To it again. We must exasperate the independent spirits in all countries—excite philosophic rage all over Europe make liberalism foam at the mouth—raise all that is wild and noisy against Rome. To effect this, we must proclaim in the face of the world these three propositions. 1. It is abominable to assert that a man may be saved in any faith whatever, provided his morals be pure. 2. It is odious and absurd to grant liberty of conscience to the people. 3. The liberty of the press cannot be held in too much horror.24

"We must bring the Pap-fed man to declare these propositions in every respect orthodox—show him their good effect upon despotic governments—upon true Catholics, the muzzlers of the people. He will fall into the snare. The propositions once published, the storm will burst forth. A general rising against Rome—a wide schism—the sacred college divided into three parties. One approves—the other blames—the third trembles. The Sick Man, still more frightened than he is now at having allowed the destruction of Poland, will shrink from the clamors, reproaches, threats, and violent ruptures that he has occasioned.

"That is well—and goes far.

"Then, set the Pope to shaking the conscience of the Sick Man, to disturb his mind, and terrify his soul.

"To sum up. Make everything bitter to him—divide his council—isolate him—frighten him—redouble the ferocious ardor of good Albini—revive the appetite of the Sanfedists[25]—give them a gulf of liberals—let there be pillage, rape, massacre, as at Cesena—a downright river of Carbonaro blood—the Sick Man will have a surfeit of it. So many butcheries in his name—he will shrink, be sure he will shrink—every day will have its remorse, every night its terror, every minute its anguish; and the abdication he already threatens will come at last—perhaps too soon. That is now the only danger; you must provide against it.

"In case of an abdication, the grand penitentiary has understood me. Instead of confiding to a general the direction of our Order, the best militia of the Holy See, I should command it myself. Thenceforward this militia would give me no uneasiness. For instance: the Janissaries and the Praetorian Guards were always fatal to authority—why?—because they were able to organize themselves as defenders of the government, independently of the government; hence their power of intimidation.

"Clement XIV. was a fool. To brand and abolish our Company was an absurd fault. To protect and make it harmless, by declaring himself the General of the Order, is what he should have done. The Company, then at his mercy, would have consented to anything. He would have absorbed us, made us vassals of the Holy See, and would no longer have had to fear our services. Clement XIV. died of the cholic. Let him heed who hears. In a similar case, I should not die the same death."

Just then, the clear and liquid voice of Rose-Pompon was again heard. Rodin bounded with rage upon his seat; but soon, as he listened to the following verse, new to him (for, unlike Philemon's widow, he had not his Beranger at his fingers' ends), the Jesuit, accessible to certain odd, superstitious notions, was confused and almost frightened at so singular a coincidence. It is Beranger's Good Pope who speaks—

>"What are monarchs? sheepish sots!
>Or they're robbers, puffed with pride,
>Wearing badges of crime blots,
>Till their certain graves gape wide.
>If they'll pour out coin for me,
>I'll absolve them—skin and bone!
>If they haggle—they shall see,
>My nieces dancing on their throne!
>So laugh away!
>Leap, my fay!
>Only watch one hurt the thunder
>First of all by Zeus under,
>I'm the Pope, the whole world's wonder!"

Rodin, half-risen from his chair, with outstretched neck and attentive eye, was still listening, when Rose-Pompon, flitting like a bee from flower to flower of her repertoire, had already begun the delightful air of Colibri. Hearing no more, the Jesuit reseated himself, in a sort of stupor; but, after some minutes' reflection, his countenance again brightened up, and he seemed to see a lucky omen in this singular incident. He resumed his pen, and the first words he wrote partook, as it were, of this strange confidence in fate.

"I have never had more hope of success than at this moment. Another reason to neglect nothing. Every presentiment demands redoubled zeal. A new thought occurred to me yesterday.

"We shall act here in concert. I have founded an ultra-Catholic paper called Neighborly Love. From its ultramontane, tyrannical, liberticidal fury, it will be thought the organ of Rome. I will confirm these reports. They will cause new terrors.

"That will be well.

"I shall raise the question of the liberty of instruction. The raw liberals will support us. Like fools, they admit us to equal rights; when our privileges, our influence of the confessional, our obedience to Rome, all place us beyond the circle of equal rights, by the advantages which we enjoy. Double fools! they think us disarmed, because they have disarmed themselves towards us.

"A burning question—irritating clamors—new cause of disgust for the Weak Man. Every little makes a mickle.

"That also is very well.

"To sum up all in two words. The end is abdication—the means, vexation, incessant torture. The Rennepont inheritance wilt pay for the election. The price agreed, the merchandise will be sold."

Rodin here paused abruptly, thinking he had heard some noise at that door of his, which opened on the staircase; therefore he listened with suspended breath; but all remaining silent, he thought he must have been deceived, and took up his pen:

"I will take care of the Rennepont business—the hinge on which will turn our temporal operations. We must begin from the foundation—substitute the play of interests, and the springs of passion, for the stupid club law of Father d'Aigrigny. He nearly compromised everything—and yet he has good parts, knows the world, has powers of seduction, quick insight—but plays ever in a single key, and is not great enough to make himself little. In his stead, I shall know how to make use of him. There is good stuff in the man. I availed myself in time of the full powers given by the R. F. G.; I may inform Father d'Aigrigny, in case of need, of the secret engagements taken by the General towards myself. Until now, I have let him invent for this inheritance the destination that you know of. A good thought, but unseasonable. The same end, by other means.

"The information was false. There are over two hundred millions. Should the eventuality occur, what was doubtful must become certain. An immense latitude is left us. The Rennepont business is now doubly mine, and within three months, the two hundred millions will be ours, by the free will of the heirs themselves. It must be so; for this failing, the temporal part would escape me, and my chances be diminished by one half. I have asked for full powers; time presses, and I act as if I had them. One piece of information is indispensable for the success of my projects. I expect it from you, and I must have it; do you understand me? The powerful influence of your brother at the Court of Vienna will serve you in this. I wish to have the most precise details as to the present position of the Duke de Reichstadt— the Napoleon II. of the Imperialists. Is it possible, by means of your brother, to open a secret correspondence with the prince, unknown to his attendants?

"Look to this promptly. It is urgent. This note will be sent off to day. I shall complete it to-morrow. It will reach you, as usual, by the hands of the petty shopkeeper."

At the moment when Rodin was sealing this letter within a double envelope, he thought that he again heard a noise at the door. He listened. After some silence, several knocks were distinctly audible. Rodin started. It was the first time any one had knocked at his door, since nearly a twelve-month that he occupied this room. Hastily placing the letter in his great-coat pocket, the Jesuit opened the old trunk under his bed, took from it a packet of papers wrapped in a tattered cotton handkerchief, added to them the two letters in cipher he had just received, and carefully relocked the trunk. The knocking continued without, and seemed to show more and more impatience. Rodin took the greengrocer's basket in his hand, tucked his umbrella under his arm, and went with some uneasiness to ascertain who was this unexpected visitor. He opened the door, and found himself face to face with Rose-Pompon, the troublesome singer, and who now, with a light and pretty courtesy, said to him in the most guileless manner in the world, "M. Rodin, if you please?"

[23] On page 110 of Lamennais' Affaires de Rome, will be seen the following admirable scathing of Rome by the most truly evangelical spirit of our age: "So long as the issue of the conflict between Poland and her oppressors remained in the balances, the papal official organ contained not one word to offend the so long victorious nation; but hardly had she gone down under the Czar's atrocious vengeance, and the long torture of a whole land doomed to rack, and exile, and servitude began, than this same journal found no language black enough to stain those whom fortune had fled. Yet it is wrong to charge this unworthy insult to papal power; it only cringes to the law which Russia lays down to it, when it says:

"'If you want to keep your own bones unbroken, bide where you are, beside the scaffold, and, as the victims pass, hoot at them!'"

[24] See Pope Gregory XVI.'s Encyclical Letter to the Bishops in France, 1832.

[25] Hardly had the Sixteenth Gregory ascended the pontifical throne, than news came of the rising in Bologna. His first idea was to call the Austrians, and incite the Sanfedist volunteer bands of fanatics. Cardinal Albini defeated the liberals at Cesena, where his followers pillaged churches, sacked the town, and ill-treated women. At Forli, cold-blooded murders were committed. In 1832 the Sanfedists (Holy Faithites) openly paraded their medals, bearing the heads of the Duke of Modena and the Pope; letters issued by the apostolic confederation; privileges and indulgences. They took the following oath: "I. A. B., vow to rear the throne and altar over the bones of infamous freedom shriekers, and exterminate these latter without pity for children's cries and women's tears." The disorders perpetrated by these marauders went beyond all bounds; the Romish Court regularized anarchy and organized the Sanfedists into volunteer corps, to which fresh privileges were granted. [Revue deux Mondes, Nov. 15th, 1844.—"La Revolution en Italie."]

CHAPTER XXXI.

FRIENDLY SERVICES.

Notwithstanding his surprise and uneasiness, Rodin did not frown. He began by locking his door after him, as he noticed the young girl's inquisitive glance. Then he said to her good-naturedly, "Who do you want, my dear?"

"M. Rodin," repeated Rose-Pompon, stoutly, opening her bright blue eyes to their full extent, and looking Rodin full in the face.

"It's not here," said he, moving towards the stairs. "I do not know him. Inquire above or below."

"No, you don't! giving yourself airs at your age!" said Rose-Pompon, shrugging her shoulders. "As if we did not know that you are M. Rodin."

"Charlemagne," said the socius, bowing; "Charlemagne, to serve you—if I am able."

"You are not able," answered Rose-Pompon, majestically; then she added with a mocking air, "So, we have our little pussy-cat hiding-places; we change our name; we are afraid Mamma Rodin will find us out."

"Come, my dear child," said the socius, with a paternal smile; "you have come to the right quarter. I am an old man, but I love youth—happy, joyous youth! Amuse yourself, pray, at my expense. Only let me pass, for I am in a hurry." And Rodin again advanced towards the stairs.

"M. Rodin," said Rose-Pompon, in a solemn voice, "I have very important things to say to you, and advice to ask about a love affair."

"Why, little madcap that you are! have you nobody to tease in your own house, that you must come here?"

"I lodge in this house, M. Rodin," answered Rose-Pompon, laying a malicious stress on the name of her victim.

"You? Oh, dear, only to think I did not know I had such a pretty neighbor."

"Yes, I have lodged here six months, M. Rodin."

"Really! where?"

"On the third story, front, M. Rodin."

"It was you, then, that sang so well just now?"

"Rather."

"You gave me great pleasure, I must say."

"You are very polite, M. Rodin."

"You lodge, I suppose, with your respectable family?"

"I believe you, M. Rodin," said Rose-Pompon, casting down her eyes with a timid air. "I lodge with Grandpapa Philemon, and Grandmamma Bacchanal—who is a queen and no mistake."

Rodin had hitherto been seriously uneasy, not knowing in what manner Rose had discovered his real name. But on hearing her mention the Bacchanal queen, with the information that she lodged in the house, he found something to compensate for the disagreeable incident of Rose-Pompon's appearance. It was, indeed, important to Rodin to find out the Bacchanal Queen, the mistress of Sleepinbuff, and the sister of Mother Bunch, who had been noted as dangerous since her interview with the superior of the convent, and the part she had taken in the projected escape of Mdlle. de Cardoville. Moreover, Rodin hoped—thanks to what he had just heard—to bring Rose-Pompon to confess to him the name of the person from whom she had learned that "Charlemagne" masked "Rodin."

Hardly had the young girl pronounced the name of the Bacchanal queen, than Rodin clasped his hands, and appeared as much surprised as interested.

"Oh, my dear child," he exclaimed, "I conjure you not to jest on this subject. Are you speaking of a young girl who bears that nickname, the sister of a deformed needlewoman."

"Yes, sir, the Bacchanal Queen is her nickname," said Rose-Pompon, astonished in her turn; "she is really Cephyse Soliveau, and she is my friend."

"Oh! she is your friend?" said Rodin, reflecting.

"Yes, sir, my bosom friend."

"So you love her?"

"Like a sister. Poor girl! I do what I can for her, and that's not much. But how comes it that a respectable man of your age should know the Bacchanal Queen?—Ah! that shows you have a false name!"

"My dear child, I am no longer inclined to laugh," said Rodin, with so sorrowful an air, that Rose-Pompon, reproaching herself with her pleasantry, said to him: "But how comes it that you know Cephyse?"

"Alas! I do not know her—but a young fellow, that I like excessively—"

"Jacques Rennepont?"

"Otherwise called Sleepinbuff. He is now in prison for debt," sighed Rodin. "I saw him yesterday."

"You saw him yesterday?—how strange!" said Rose-Pompon, clapping her hands. "Quick! quick!—come over to Philemon's, to give Cephyse news of her lover. She is so uneasy about him."

"My dear child, I should like to give her good news of that worthy fellow, whom I like in spite of his follies, for who has not been guilty of follies?" added Rodin, with indulgent good-nature.

"To be sure," said Rose-Pompon, twisting about as if she still wore the costume of a debardeur.

"I will say more," added Rodin: "I love him because of his follies; for, talk as we may, my dear child, there is always something good at bottom, a good heart, or something, in those who spend generously their money for other people."

"Well, come! you are a very good sort of a man," said Rose-Pompon, enchanted with Rodin's philosophy. "But why will you not come and see Cephyse, and talk to her of Jacques?"

"Of what use would it be to tell her what she knows already—that Jacques is in prison? What I should like, would be to get the worthy fellow out of his scrape."

"Oh, sir! only do that, only get Jacques out of prison," cried Rose Pompon, warmly, "and we will both give you a kiss—me and Cephyse!"

"It would be throwing kisses away, dear little madcap!" said Rodin, smiling. "But be satisfied, I want no reward to induce me to do good when I can."

"Then you hope to get Jacques out of prison?"

Rodin shook his head, and answered with a grieved and disappointed air. "I did hope it. Certainly, I did hope it; but now all is changed."

"How's that?" asked Rose-Pompon, with surprise.

"That foolish joke of calling me M. Rodin may appear very amusing to you, my dear child. I understand it, you being only an echo. Some one has said to you: 'Go and tell M. Charlemagne that he is one M. Rodin. That will be very funny.'"

"Certainly, I should never myself have thought of calling you M. Rodin. One does not invent such names," answered Rose-Pompon.

"Well! that person with his foolish jokes, has done, without knowing it, a great injury to Jacques Rennepont."

"What! because I called you Rodin instead of Charlemagne?" cried Rose Pompon, much regretting the pleasantry which she had carried on at the instigation of Ninny Moulin. "But really, sir," she added, "what can this joke have to do with the service that you were, about to render Jacques?"

"I am not at liberty to tell you, my child. In truth, I am very sorry for poor Jacques. Believe me, I am; but do let me pass.

"Listen to me, sir, I beg," said Rose-Pompon; "if I told you the name of the person who told me to call you Rodin, would you interest yourself again for Jacques?"

"I do not wish to know any one's secrets, my dear child. In all this, you have been the echo of persons who are, perhaps, very dangerous; and, notwithstanding the interest I feel for Jacques Rennepont, I do not wish, you understand, to make myself enemies. Heaven forbid!"

Rose-Pompon did not at all comprehend Rodin's fears, and upon this he had counted; for after a second's reflection, the young girl resumed: "Well, sir—this is too deep for me; I do not understand it. All I know is, that I am truly sorry if I have injured a good young man by a mere joke. I will tell you exactly how it happened. My frankness may be of some use."

"Frankness will often clear up the most obscure matters," said Rodin, sententiously.

"After all," said Rose-Pompon, "it's Ninny's fault. Why does he tell me nonsense, that might injure poor Cephyse's lover? You see, sir, it happened in this way. Ninny Moulin who is fond of a joke, saw you just now in the street. The portress told him that your name was Charlemagne. He said to me: 'No; his name is Rodin. We must play him a trick. Go to his room, Rose-Pompon, knock at the door, and call him M. Rodin. You will see what a rum face he will make.' I promised Ninny Moulin not to name him; but I do it, rather than run the risk of injuring Jacques."

At Ninny Moulin's name Rodin had not been able to repress a movement of surprise. This pamphleteer, whom he had employed to edit the "Neighborly Love," was not personally formidable; but, being fond of talking in his drink, he might become troublesome, particularly if Rodin, as was probable, had often to visit this house, to execute his project upon Sleepinbuff, through the medium of the Bacchanal Queen. The socius resolved, therefore, to provide against this inconvenience.

"So, my dear child," said he to Rose-Pompon, "it is a M. Desmoulins that persuaded you to play off this silly joke?"

"Not Desmoulins, but Dumoulin," corrected Rose. "He writes in the pewholders' papers, and defends the saints for money; for, if Ninny Moulin is a saint, his patrons are Saint Drinkard and Saint Flashette, as he himself declares."

"This gentleman appears to be very gay."

"Oh! a very good fellow."

"But stop," resumed Rodin, appearing to recollect himself; "ain't he a man about thirty-six or forty, fat, with a ruddy complexion?"

"Ruddy as a glass of red wine," said Rose-Pompon, "and with a pimpled nose like a mulberry."

"That's the man—M. Dumoulin. Oh! in that case, I am quite satisfied, my dear child. The jest no longer makes me uneasy; for M. Dumoulin is a very worthy man—only perhaps a little too fond of his joke."

"Then, sir, you will try to be useful to Jacques? The stupid pleasantry of Ninny Moulin will not prevent you?"

"I hope not."

"But I must not tell Ninny Moulin that you know it was he who sent me to call you M. Rodin—eh, sir?"

"Why not? In every case, my dear child, it is always better to speak frankly the truth."

"But, sir, Ninny Moulin so strongly recommended me not to name him to you—"

"If you have named him, it is from a very good motive; why not avow it? However, my dear child, this concerns you, not me. Do as you think best."

"And may I tell Cephyse of your good intentions towards Jacques?"

"The truth, my dear child, always the truth. One need never hesitate to say what is."

"Poor Cephyse! how happy she will be!" cried Rose-Pompon, cheerfully; "and the news will come just in time."

"Only you must not exaggerate; I do not promise positively to get this good fellow out of prison; I say, that I will do what I can. But what I promise positively is—for, since the imprisonment of poor Jacques, your friend must be very much straitened—"

"Alas, sir!"

"What I promise positively is some little assistance which your friend will receive to-day, to enable her to live honestly; and if she behaves well—hereafter—why, hereafter, we shall see."

"Oh, sir! you do not know how welcome will be your assistance to poor Cephyse! One might fancy you were her actual good angel. Faith! you may call yourself Rodin, or Charlemagne; all I know is, that you are a nice, sweet—"

"Come, come, do not exaggerate," said Rodin; "say a good sort of old fellow; nothing more, my dear child. But see how things fall out, sometimes! Who could have told me, when I heard you knock at my door—which, I must say, vexed me a great deal—that it was a pretty little neighbor of mine, who under the pretext of playing off a joke, was to put me in the way of doing a good action? Go and comfort your friend; this evening she will receive some assistance; and let us have hope and confidence. Thanks be, there are still some good people in the world!"

"Oh, sir! you prove it yourself."

"Not at all! The happiness of the old is to see the young happy."

This was said by Rodin with so much apparent kindness, that Rose-Pompon felt the tears well up to her eyes, and answered with much emotion: "Sir, Cephyse and me are only poor girls; there are many more virtuous in the world; but I venture to say, we have good hearts. Now, if ever you should be ill, only send for us; there are no Sisters of Charity that will take better care of you. It is all that we can offer you, without reckoning Philemon, who shall go through fire and water for you, I give you my word for it—and Cephyse, I am sure, will answer for Jacques also, that he will be yours in life and death."

"You see, my dear child, that I was right in saying—a fitful head and a good heart. Adieu, till we meet again."

Thereupon Rodin, taking up the basket, which he had placed on the ground by the side of his umbrella, prepared to descend the stairs.

"First of all, you must give me this basket; it will be in your way going down," said Rose-Pompon, taking the basket from the hands of Rodin, notwithstanding his resistance. Then she added: "Lean upon my arm. The stairs are so dark. You might slip."

"I will accept your offer, my dear child, for I am not very courageous." Leaning paternally on the right arm of Rose-Pompon, who held the basket in her left hand, Rodin descended the stairs, and crossed the court-yard.

"Up there, on the third story, do you see that big face close to the window-frame?" said Rose-Pompon suddenly to Rodin, stopping in the centre of the little court. "That is my Ninny Moulin. Do you know him? Is he the same as yours?"

"The same as mine," said Rodin, raising his head, and waving his hand very affectionately to Jacques Dumoulin, who, stupefied thereat, retired abruptly from the window.

"The poor fellow! I am sure he is afraid of me since his foolish joke," said Rodin, smiling. "He is very wrong."

And he accompanied these last words with a sinister nipping of the lips, not perceived by Rose-Pompon.

"And now, my dear child," said he, as they both entered the passage, "I no longer need you assistance; return to your friend, and tell her the good news you have heard."

"Yes, sir, you are right. I burn with impatience to tell her what a good man you are." And Rose-Pompon sprung towards the stairs.

"Stop, stop! how about my basket that the little madcap carries off with her?" said Rodin.

"Oh true! I beg your pardon, sir. Poor Cephyse! how pleased she will be. Adieu, sir!" And Rose-Pompon's pretty figure disappeared in the darkness of the staircase, which she mounted with an alert and impatient step.

Rodin issued from the entry. "Here is your basket, my good lady," said he, stopping at the threshold of Mother Arsene's shop. "I give you my humble thanks for your kindness."

"For nothing, my dear sir, for nothing. It is all at your service. Well, was the radish good?"

"Succulent, my dear madame, and excellent."

"Oh! I am glad of it. Shall we soon see you again?"

"I hope so. But could you tell me where is the nearest post-office?"

"Turn to the left, the third house, at the grocer's."

"A thousand thanks."

"I wager it's a love letter for your sweetheart," said Mother Arsene, enlivened probably by Rose Pompon's and Ninny Moulin's proximity.

"Ha! ha! ha! the good lady!" said Rodin, with a titter. Then, suddenly resuming his serious aspect, he made a low bow to the greengrocer, adding: "Your most obedient humble servant!" and walked out into the street.

We now usher the reader into Dr. Baleinier's asylum, in which Mdlle. de Cardoville was confined.

CHAPTER XXXII.

THE ADVICE.

Adrienne de Cardoville had been still more strictly confined in Dr. Baleinier's house, since the double nocturnal attempt of Agricola and Dagobert, in which the soldier, though severely wounded, had succeeded, thanks to the intrepid devotion of his son, seconded by the heroic Spoil sport, in gaining the little garden gate of the convent, and escaping by way of the boulevard, along with the young smith. Four o'clock had just struck. Adrienne, since the previous day, had been removed to a chamber on the second story of the asylum. The grated window, with closed shutters, only admitted a faint light to this apartment. The young lady, since her interview with Mother Bunch, expected to be delivered any day by the intervention of her friends. But she felt painful uneasiness on the subject of Agricola and Dagobert, being absolutely ignorant of the issue of the struggle in which her intended liberators had been engaged with the people of the asylum and convent. She had in vain questioned her keepers on the subject; they had remained perfectly mute. These new incidents had augmented the bitter resentment of Adrienne against the Princess de Saint Dizier, Father d'Aigrigny, and their creatures. The slight paleness of Mdlle. de Cardoville's charming face, and her fine eyes a little drooping, betrayed her recent sufferings; seated before a little table, with her forehead resting upon one of her hands, half veiled by the long curls of her golden hair, she was turning over the leaves of a book. Suddenly, the door opened, and M. Baleinier entered. The doctor, a Jesuit, in lay attire, a docile and passive instrument of the will of his Order, was only half in the confidence of Father d'Aigrigny and the Princess de Saint-Dizier. He was ignorant of the object of the imprisonment of Mdlle. de Cardoville; he was ignorant also of the sudden change which had taken place in the relative position of Father d'Aigrigny and Rodin, after the reading of the testament of Marius de Rennepont. The doctor had, only the day before, received orders from Father d'Aigrigny (now acting under the directions of Rodin) to confine Mdlle. de Cardoville still more strictly, to act towards her with redoubled severity, and to endeavor to force her, it will be seen by what expedients, to renounce the judicial proceedings, which she promised herself to take hereafter against her persecutors. At sight of the doctor, Mdlle. de Cardoville could not hide the aversion and disdain with which this man inspired her. M. Baleinier, on the contrary, always smiling, always courteous, approached Adrienne with perfect ease and confidence, stopped a few steps from her, as if to study her features more attentively, and then added like a man who is satisfied with the observations he had made: "Come! the unfortunate events of the night before last have had a less injurious influence than I feared. There is some improvement; the complexion is less flushed, the look calmer, the eyes still somewhat too bright, but no longer shining with such unnatural fire. You are getting on so well! Now the cure must be prolonged—for this unfortunate night affair threw you into a state of excitement, that was only the more dangerous from your not being conscious of it. Happily, with care, your recovery will not, I hope, be very much delayed." Accustomed though she was to the audacity of this tool of the Congregation, Mdlle. de Cardoville could not forbear saying to him, with a smile of bitter disdain: "What impudence, sir, there is in your probity! What effrontery in your zeal to earn your hire! Never for a moment do you lay aside your mask; craft and falsehood are ever on your lips. Really, if this shameful comedy causes you as much fatigue as it does me disgust and contempt, they can never pay you enough."

"Alas!" said the doctor, in a sorrowful tone; "always this unfortunate delusion, that you are not in want of our care!—that I am playing a part, when I talk to you of the sad state in which you were when we were obliged to bring you hither by stratagem. Still, with the exception of this little sign of rebellious insanity, your condition has marvellously improved. You are on the high-road to a complete cure. By-and-by, your excellent heart will render me the justice that is due to me; and, one day, I shall be judged as I deserve."

"I, believe it, sir; the day approaches, in which you will be judged as you deserve," said Adrienne, laying great stress upon the two words.

"Always that other fixed idea," said the doctor with a sort of commiseration. "Come, be reasonable. Do not think of this childishness."

"What! renounce my intention to demand at the hands of justice reparation for myself, and disgrace for you and your accomplices? Never, sir—never!"

"Well!" said the doctor, shrugging his shoulders; "once at liberty, thank heaven, you will have many other things to think of, my fair enemy."

"You forget piously the evil that you do; but I, sir, have a better memory."

"Let us talk seriously. Have you really the intention of applying to the courts?" inquired Dr. Baleinier, in a grave tone.

"Yes, sir, and you know that what I intend, I firmly carry out."

"Well! I can only conjure you not to follow out this idea," replied the doctor, in a still more solemn tone; "I ask it as a favor, in the name of your own interest."

"I think, sir, that you are a little too ready to confound your interest with mine."

"Now come," said Dr. Baleinier, with a feigned impatience, as if quite certain of convincing Mdlle. de Cardoville on the instant; "would you have the melancholy courage to plunge into despair two persons full of goodness and generosity?"

"Only two? The jest would be complete, if you were to reckon three: you, sir, and my aunt, and Abbe d'Aigrigny; for these are no doubt the generous persons in whose name you implore my pity."

"No, madame; I speak neither of myself, nor of your aunt, nor of Abbe d'Aigrigny."

"Of whom, then, sir?" asked Mdlle. de Cardoville with surprise.

"Of two poor fellows, who, no doubt sent by those whom you call your friends, got into the neighboring convent the other night, and thence into this garden. The guns which you heard go off were fired at them."

"Alas! I thought so. They refused to tell me if either of them was wounded," said Adrienne, with painful emotion.

"One of them received a wound, but not very serious, since he was able to fly and escape pursuit."

"Thank God!" cried Mdlle. de Cardoville, clasping her hands with fervor.

"It is quite natural that you should rejoice at their escape, but by what strange contradiction do you now wish to put the officers of justice on their track? A singular manner, truly, of rewarding their devotion!"

"What do you say, sir?" asked Mdlle. de Cardoville.

"For if they should be arrested," resumed Dr. Baleinier, without answering her, "as they have been guilty of housebreaking and attempted burglary, they would be sent to the galleys."

"Heavens! and for my sake!"

"Yes; it would be for you, and what is worse, by you, that they would be condemned."

"By me, sir?"

"Certainly; that is, if you follow up your vengeance against your aunt and Abbe d'Aigrigny—I do not speak of myself, for I am quite safe; in a word, if you persist in laying your complaint before the magistrates, that you have been unjustly confined in this house."

"I do not understand you, sir. Explain yourself," said Adrienne, with growing uneasiness.

"Child that you are!" cried the Jesuit of the short robe, with an air of conviction; "do you think that if the law once takes cognizance of this affair, you can stop short its action where and when you please? When you leave this house, you lodge a complaint against me and against your family; well, what happens? The law interferes, inquires, calls witnesses, enters into the most minute investigations. Then, what follows? Why, that this nocturnal escalade, which the superior of the convent has some interest in hushing up, for fear of scandal—that this nocturnal attempt, I say, which I also would keep quiet, is necessarily divulged, and as it involves a serious crime, to which a heavy penalty is attached, the law will ferret into it, and find out these unfortunate men, and if, as is probable, they are detained in Paris by their duties or occupations, or even by a false security, arising from the honorable motives which they know to have actuated them, they will be arrested. And who will be the cause of this arrest? You, by your deposition against us."

"Oh, sir! that would be horrible; but it is impossible."

"It is very possible, on the contrary," returned M. Baleinier: "so that, while I and the superior of the convent, who alone are really entitled to complain, only wish to keep quiet this unpleasant affair, it is you—you, for whom these unfortunate men have risked the galleys—that will deliver them up to justice."

Though Mdlle. de Cardoville was not completely duped by the lay Jesuit, she guessed that the merciful intentions which he expressed with regard to Dagobert and his son, would be absolutely subordinate to the course she might take in pressing or abandoning the legitimate vengeance which she meant to claim of authority. Indeed, Rodin, whose instructions the doctor was following without knowing it, was too cunning to have it said to Mdlle. de Cardoville: "If you attempt any proceedings, we denounce Dagobert and his son;" but he attained the same end, by inspiring Adrienne with fears on the subject of her two liberators, so as to prevent her taking any hostile measures. Without knowing the exact law on the subject, Mdlle. de Cardoville had too much good sense not to understand that Dagobert and Agricola might be very seriously involved in consequence of their nocturnal adventure, and might even find themselves in a terrible position. And yet, when she thought of all she had suffered in that house, and of all the just resentment she entertained in the bottom of her heart, Adrienne felt unwilling to renounce the stern pleasure of exposing such odious machinations to the light of day. Dr. Baleinier watched with sullen attention her whom he considered his dupe, for he thought he could divine the cause of the silence and hesitation of Mdlle. de Cardoville.

"But, sir," resumed the latter, unable to conceal her anxiety, "if I were disposed, for whatever reason, to make no complaint, and to forget the wrongs I have suffered, when should I leave this place?"

"I cannot tell; for I do not know when you will be radically cured," said the doctor, benignantly. "You are in a very good way, but—"

"Still this insolent and stupid acting!" broke forth Mdlle. de Cardoville, interrupting the doctor with indignation. "I ask, and if it must be, I entreat you to tell me how long I am to be shut up in this dreadful house, for I shall leave it some day, I suppose?"

"I hope so, certainly," said the Jesuit of the short robe, with unction; "but when, I am unable to say. Moreover, I must tell you frankly, that every precaution is taken against such attempts as those of the other night; and the most vigorous watch will be maintained, to prevent your communicating with any one. And all this in your own interest, that your poor head may not again be dangerously excited."

"So, sir," said Adrienne, almost terrified, "compared with what awaits me, the last few days have been days of liberty."

"Your interest before everything," answered the doctor, in a fervent tone.

Mdlle. de Cardoville, feeling the impotence of her indignation and despair, heaved a deep sigh, and hid her face in her hands.

At this moment, quick footsteps were heard in the passage, and one of the nurses entered, after having knocked at the door.

"Sir," said she to the doctor, with a frightened air, "there are two gentlemen below, who wish to see you instantly, and the lady also."

Adrienne raised her head hastily; her eyes were bathed in tears.

"What are the names of these persons?" said M. Baleinier, much astonished.

"One of them said to me," answered the nurse: "'Go and inform Dr. Baleinier that I am a magistrate, and that I come on a duty regarding Mdlle. de Cardoville.'"

"A magistrate!" exclaimed the Jesuit of the short robe, growing purple in the face, and unable to hide his surprise and uneasiness.

"Heaven be praised!" cried Adrienne, rising with vivacity, her countenance beaming through her tears with hope and joy; "my friends have been informed in time, and the hour of justice is arrived!"

"Ask these persons to walk up," said Dr. Baleinier, after a moment's reflection. Then, with a still more agitated expression of countenance, he approached Adrienne with a harsh, and almost menacing air, which contrasted with the habitual placidity of his hypocritical smile, and said to her in a low voice: "Take care, madame! do not rejoice too soon."

"I no longer fear you," answered Mdlle. de Cardoville, with a bright, flashing eye. "M. de Montbron is no doubt returned to Paris, and has been informed in time. He accompanies the magistrate, and comes to deliver me. I pity you, sir—both you and yours," added Adrienne, with an accent of bitter irony.

"Madame," cried M. Baleinier, no longer able to dissemble his growing alarm, "I repeat to you, take care! Remember what I have told you. Your accusations would necessarily involve the discovery of what took place the other night. Beware! the fate of the soldier and his son is in your hands. Recollect they are in danger of the convict's chains."

"Oh! I am not your dupe, sir. You are holding out a covert menace. Have at least the courage to say to me, that, if I complain to the magistrates, you will denounce the soldier and his son."

"I repeat, that, if you make any complaint, those two people are lost," answered the doctor, ambiguously.

Startled by what was really dangerous in the doctor's threats, Adrienne asked: "Sir, if this magistrate questions me, do you think I will tell him a falsehood?"

"You will answer what is true," said M. Baleinier, hastily, in the hope of still attaining his end. "You will answer that you were in so excited a state of mind a few days ago, that it was thought advisable, for your own sake, to bring you hither, without your knowing it. But you are now so much better, that you acknowledge the utility of the measures taken with regard to you. I will confirm these words for, after all, it is the truth."

"Never!" cried Mdlle. de Cardoville, with indignation, "never will I be the accomplice of so infamous a falsehood; never will I be base enough to justify the indignities that I have suffered!"

"Here is the magistrate," said M. Baleinier, as he caught the sound of approaching footsteps. "Beware!"

The door opened, and, to the indescribable amazement of the doctor, Rodin appeared on the threshold, accompanied by a man dressed in black, with a dignified and severe countenance. In the interest of his projects, and from motives of craft and prudence that will hereafter be known, Rodin had not informed Father d'Aigrigny, and consequently the doctor, of the unexpected visit he intended to pay to the asylum, accompanied by a magistrate. On the contrary, he had only the day before given orders to M. Baleinier to confine Mdlle. de Cardoville still more strictly. Therefore, imagine the stupor of the doctor when he saw the judicial officer, whose unexpected presence and imposing aspect were otherwise sufficiently alarming, enter the room, accompanied by Rodin, Abbe d'Aigrigny's humble and obscure secretary. From the door, Rodin, who was very shabbily dressed, as usual, pointed out Mdlle. de Cardoville to the magistrate, by a gesture at once respectful and compassionate. Then, while the latter, who had not been able to repress a movement of admiration at sight of the rare beauty of Adrienne, seemed to examine her with as much surprise as interest, the Jesuit modestly receded several steps.

Dr. Baleinier in his extreme astonishment, hoping to be understood by Rodin, made suddenly several private signals, as if to interrogate him on the cause of the magistrate's visit. But this was only productive of fresh amazement to M. Baleinier; for Rodin did not appear to recognize him, or to understand his expressive pantomime, and looked at him with affected bewilderment. At length, as the doctor, growing impatient, redoubled his mute questionings, Rodin advanced with a stride, stretched forward his crooked neck, and said, in a loud voice: "What is your pleasure, doctor?"

These words, which completely disconcerted Baleinier, broke the silence which had reigned for some seconds, and the magistrate turned round. Rodin added, with imperturbable coolness: "Since our arrival, the doctor has been making all sorts of mysterious signs to me. I suppose he has something private to communicate, but, as I have no secrets, I must beg him to speak out loud."

This reply, so embarrassing for M. Baleinier, uttered in a tone of aggression, and with an air of icy coldness, plunged the doctor into such new and deep amazement, that he remained for some moments without answering. No doubt the magistrate was struck with this incident, and with the silence which followed it, for he cast a look of great severity on the doctor. Mdlle. de Cardoville, who had expected to have seen M. de Montbron, was also singularly surprised.

CHAPTER XXXIII.

THE ACCUSER.

Baleinier, disconcerted for a moment by the unexpected presence of a magistrate, and by Rodin's inexplicable attitude, soon recovered his presence of mind, and addressing his colleague of the longer robe, said to him: "If I make signs to you, sir, it was that, while I wished to respect the silence which this gentleman"—glancing at the magistrate—"has preserved since his entrance, I desired to express my surprise at the unexpected honor of this visit."

"It is to the lady that I will explain the reason for my silence, and beg her to excuse it," replied the magistrate, as he made a half-bow to Adrienne, whom he thus continued to address: "I have just received so serious a declaration with regard to you, madame, that I could not forbear looking at you for a moment in silence, to see if I could read in your countenance or in your attitude, the truth or falsehood of the accusation that has been placed in my hands; and I have every reason to believe that it is but too well founded."

"May I at length be informed, sir," said Dr. Baleinier, in a polite but firm tone, "to whom I have the honor of speaking?"

"Sir, I am juge d'instruction, and I have come to inform myself as to a fact which has been pointed out to me—"

"Will you do me the honor to explain yourself, sir?" said the doctor, bowing.

"Sir," resumed the magistrate, M. de Gernande, a man of about fifty years of age, full of firmness and straightforwardness, and knowing how to unite the austere duties of his position with benevolent politeness, "you are accused of having committed—a very great error, not to use a harsher expression. As for the nature of that error, I prefer believing, sir, that you (a first rate man of science) may have been deceived in the calculation of a medical case, rather than suspect you of having forgotten all that is sacred in the exercise of a profession that is almost a priesthood."

"When you specify the facts, sir," answered the Jesuit of the short robe, with a degree of haughtiness, "it will be easy for me to prove that my reputation as a man of science is no less free from reproach, than my conscience as a man of honor."

"Madame," said M. de Gernande, addressing Adrienne, "is it true that you were conveyed to this house by stratagem?"

"Sir," cried M. Baleinier, "permit me to observe, that the manner in which you open this question is an insult to me."

"Sir, it is to the lady that I have the honor of addressing myself," replied M. de Gernande, sternly; "and I am the sole judge of the propriety of my questions."

Adrienne was about to answer affirmatively to the magistrate, when an expressive took from Dr. Baleinier reminded her that she would perhaps expose Dagobert and his son to cruel dangers. It was no base and vulgar feeling of vengeance by which Adrienne was animated, but a legitimate indignation, inspired by odious hypocrisy. She would have thought it cowardly not to unmask the criminals; but wishing to avoid compromising others, she said to the magistrate, with an accent full of mildness and dignity: "Permit me, sir, in my turn, rather to ask you a question."

"Speak, madame."

"Will the answer I make be considered a formal accusation?"

"I have come hither, madame, to ascertain the truth, and no consideration should induce you to dissemble it."

"So be it, sir," resumed Adrienne; "but suppose, having just causes of complaint, I lay them before you, in order to be allowed to leave this house, shall I afterwards be at liberty not to press the accusations I have made?"

"You may abandon proceedings, madame, but the law will take up your case in the name of society, if its rights have been inured in your person."

"Shall I then not be allowed to pardon? Should I not be sufficiently avenged by a contemptuous forgetfulness of the wrongs I have suffered?"

"Personally, madame, you may forgive and forget; but I have the honor to repeat to you, that society cannot show the same indulgence, if it should turn out that you have been the victim of a criminal machination—and I have every reason to fear it is so. The manner in which you express yourself, the generosity of your sentiments, the calmness and dignity of your attitude, convince me that I have been well informed."

"I hope, sir," said Dr. Baleinier, recovering his coolness, "that you will at least communicate the declaration that has been made to you."

"It has been declared to me, sir," said the magistrate, in a stern voice, "that Mdlle. de Cardoville was brought here by stratagem."

"By stratagem?"

"Yes, sir."

"It is true. The lady was brought here by stratagem," answered the Jesuit of the short robe, after a moment's silence.

"You confess it, then?" said M. de Gernande.

"Certainly I do, sir. I admit that I had recourse to means which we are unfortunately too often obliged to employ, when persons who most need our assistance are unconscious of their own sad state."

"But, sir," replied the magistrate, "it has also been declared to me, that Mdlle. de Cardoville never required such aid."

"That, sir, is a question of medical jurisprudence, which has to be examined and discussed," said M. Baleinier, recovering his assurance.

"It will, indeed, sir, be seriously discussed; for you are accused of confining Mdlle. De Cardoville, while in the full possession of all her faculties."

"And may I ask you for what purpose?" said M. de Baleinier, with a slight shrug of the shoulders, and in a tone of irony. "What interest had I to commit such a crime, even admitting that my reputation did not place me above so odious and absurd a charge?"

"You are said to have acted, sir, in furtherance of a family plot, devised against Mdlle. de Cardoville for a pecuniary motive."

"And who has dared, sir, to make so calumnious a charge?" cried Dr. Baleinier, with indignant warmth. "Who has had the audacity to accuse a respectable, and I dare to say, respected man, of having been the accomplice in such infamy?"

"I," said Rodin, coldly.

"You!" cried Dr. Baleinier, falling back two steps, as if thunderstruck.

"Yes, I accuse you," repeated Rodin, in a clear sharp voice.

"Yes, it was this gentleman who came to me this morning, with ample proofs, to demand my interference in favor of Mdlle. de Cardoville," said the magistrate, drawing back a little, to give Adrienne the opportunity of seeing her defender.

Throughout this scene, Rodin's name had not hitherto been mentioned. Mdlle. de Cardoville had often heard speak of the Abbe d'Aigrigny's secretary in no very favorable terms; but, never having seen him, she did not know that her liberator was this very Jesuit. She therefore looked towards him, with a glance in which were mingled curiosity, interest, surprise and gratitude. Rodin's cadaverous countenance, his repulsive ugliness, his sordid dress, would a few days before have occasioned Adrienne a perhaps invincible feeling of disgust. But the young lady, remembering how the sempstress, poor, feeble, deformed, and dressed almost in rags was endowed notwithstanding her wretched exterior, with one of the noblest and most admirable hearts, recalled this recollection in favor of the Jesuit. She forgot that he was ugly and sordid, only to remember that he was old, that he seemed poor, and that he had come to her assistance. Dr. Baleinier, notwithstanding his craft, notwithstanding his audacious hypocrisy, in spite even of his presence of mind, could not conceal how much he was disturbed by Rodin's denunciation. His head became troubled as he remembered how, on the first day of Adrienne's confinement in this house, the implacable appeal of Rodin, through the hole in the door, had prevented him (Baleinier) from yielding to emotions of pity, inspired by the despair of this unfortunate young girl, driven almost to doubt of her own reason. And yet it was this very Rodin, so cruel, so inexorable, the devoted agent of Father d'Aigrigny, who denounced him (Baleinier), and brought a magistrate to set Adrienne at liberty—when, only the day before, Father d'Aigrigny had ordered an increase of severity towards her!

The lay Jesuit felt persuaded that Rodin was betraying Father d'Aigrigny in the most shameful manner, and that Mdlle. de Cardoville's friends had bribed and bought over this scoundrelly secretary. Exasperated by what he considered a monstrous piece of treachery, the doctor exclaimed, in a voice broken with rage: "And it is you, sir, that have the impudence to accuse me—you, who only a few days ago—"

Then, reflecting that the retort upon Rodin would be self-accusation, he appeared to give way to an excess of emotion, and resumed with bitterness: "Ah, sir, you are the last person that I should have thought capable of this odious denunciation. It is shameful!"

"And who had a better right than I to denounce this infamy?" answered Rodin, in a rude, overbearing tone. "Was I not in a position to learn—unfortunately, too late—the nature of the conspiracy of which Mdlle. de Cardoville and others have been the victims? Then, what was my duty as an honest man? Why, to inform the magistrate, to prove what I set forth, and to accompany him hither. That is what I have done."

"So, sir," said the doctor, addressing the magistrate, "it is not only myself that this man accuses, but he dares also—"

"I accuse the Abbe d'Aigrigny," resumed Rodin, in a still louder and more imperative tone, interrupting the doctor, "I accuse the Princess de Saint-Dizier, I accuse you, sir—of having, from a vile motive of self interest, confined Mdlle. de Cardoville in this house, and the two daughters of Marshal Simon in the neighboring convent. Is that clear?"

"Alas! it is only too true," said Adrienne, hastily. "I have seen those poor children all in tears, making signs of distress to me."

The accusation of Rodin, with regard to the orphans, was a new and fearful blow for Dr. Baleinier. He felt perfectly convinced that the traitor had passed clear over to the enemy's camp. Wishing therefore to put an end to this embarrassing scene, he tried to put a good face on the matter, in spite of his emotion, and said to the magistrate:

"I might confine myself, sir, to silence—disdaining to answer such accusations, till a judicial decision had given them some kind of authority. But, strong in a good conscience I address myself to Mdlle. de Cardoville, and I beg her to say if this very morning I did not inform her, that her health would soon be sufficiently restored to allow her to leave this house. I conjure her, in the name of her well-known love of truth to state if such was not my language, when I was alone with her—"

"Come, sir!" said Rodin, interrupting Baleinier with an insolent air; "suppose that, from pure generosity, this dear young lady were to admit as much—what will it prove in your favor?—why, nothing at all."

"What, sir," cried the doctor, "do you presume—"

"I presume to unmask you, without asking your leave. What have you just told us? Why, that being alone with Mdlle. de Cardoville, you talked to her as if she were really mad. How very conclusive!"

"But, sir—" cried the doctor.

"But, sir," resumed Rodin, without allowing him to continue, "it is evident that, foreseeing the possibility of what has occurred to-day, and, to provide yourself with a hole to creep out at, you have pretended to believe your own execrable falsehood, in presence of this poor young lady, that you might afterwards call in aid the evidence of your own assumed conviction. Come, sir! such stories will not go down with people of common sense or common humanity."

"Come now, sir!" exclaimed Baleinier, angrily.

"Well, sir," resumed Rodin, in a still louder voice, which completely drowned that of the doctor; "is it true, or is it not, that you have recourse to the mean evasion of ascribing this odious imprisonment to a scientific error? I affirm that you do so, and that you think yourself safe, because you can now say: 'Thanks to my care, the young lady has recovered her reason. What more would you have?'"

"Yes, I do say that, sir, and I maintain it."

"You maintain a falsehood; for it is proven that the lady never lost her reason for a moment."

"But I, sir, maintain that she did lose it."

"And I, sir, will prove the contrary," said Rodin.

"You? How will you do that?" cried the doctor.

"That I shall take care not to tell you at present, as you may well suppose," answered Rodin, with an ironical smile, adding with indignation: "But, really, sir, you ought to die for shame, to dare to raise such a question in presence of the lady. You should at least have spared her this discussion."

"Sir!"

"Oh, fie, sir! I say, fie! It is odious to maintain this argument before her— odious if you speak truth, doubly odious if you lie," said Rodin, with disgust.

"This violence is inconceivable!" cried the Jesuit of the short robe, exasperated; "and I think the magistrate shows great partiality in allowing such gross calumnies to be heaped upon me!"

"Sir," answered M. de Gernande, severely, "I am entitled not only to hear, but to provoke any contradictory discussion that may enlighten me in the execution of my duty; it results from all this, that, even in your opinion, sir, Mdlle. de Cardoville's health is sufficiently good to allow her to return home immediately."

"At least, I do not see any very serious inconvenience likely to arise from it, sir," said the doctor: "only I maintain that the cure is not so complete as it might have been, and, on this subject, I decline all responsibility for the future."

"You can do so, safely," said Rodin; "it is not likely that the young lady will ever again have recourse to your honest assistance."

"It is useless, therefore, to employ my official authority, to demand the immediate liberation of Mdlle. de Cardoville," said the magistrate.

"She is free," said Baleinier, "perfectly free."

"As for the question whether you have imprisoned her on the plea of a suppositious madness, the law will inquire into it, sir, and you will be heard."

"I am quite easy, sir," answered M. Baleinier, trying to look so; "my conscience reproaches me with nothing."

"I hope it may turn out well, sir," said M. de Gernande. "However bad appearances may be, more especially when persons of your station in society are concerned, we should always wish to be convinced of their innocence." Then, turning to Adrienne, he added: "I understand, madame, how painful this scene must be to all your feelings of delicacy and generosity; hereafter, it will depend upon yourself, either to proceed for damages against M. Baleinier, or to let the law take its course. One word more. The bold and upright man"—here the magistrate pointed to Rodin—"who has taken up your cause in so frank and disinterested a manner, expressed a belief that you would, perhaps, take charge for the present of Marshal Simon's daughters, whose liberation I am about to demand from the convent where they also are confined by stratagem."

"The fact is, sir," replied Adrienne, "that, as soon as I learned the arrival of Marshal Simon's daughters in Paris, my intention was to offer them apartments in my house. These young ladies are my near relations. It is at once a duty and a pleasure for me to treat them as sisters. I shall, therefore, be doubly grateful to you, sir, if you will trust them to my care."

"I think that I cannot serve them better," answered M. de Gernande. Then, addressing Baleinier, he added, "Will you consent, sir, to my bringing these two ladies hither? I will go and fetch them, while Mdlle. de Cardoville prepares for her departure. They will then be able to leave this house with their relation."

"I entreat the lady to make use of this house as her own, until she leaves it," replied M. Baleinier. "My carriage shall be at her orders to take her home."

"Madame," said the magistrate, approaching Adrienne, "without prejudging the question, which must soon be decided by, a court of law, I may at least regret that I was not called in sooner. Your situation must have been a very cruel one."

"There will at least remain to me, sir, from this mournful time," said Adrienne, with graceful dignity, "one precious and touching remembrance—that of the interest which you have shown me. I hope that you will one day permit me to thank you, at my own home, not for the justice you have done me, but for the benevolent and paternal manner in which you have done it. And moreover, sir," added Mdlle. de Cardoville, with a sweet smile, "I should like to prove to you, that what they call my cure is complete."

M. de Gernande bowed respectfully in reply. During the abort dialogue of the magistrate with Adrienne, their backs were both turned to Baleinier and Rodin. The latter, profiting by this moment's opportunity, hastily slipped into the doctor's hand a note just written with a pencil in the bottom of his hat. Baleinier looked at Rodin in stupefied amazement. But the latter made a peculiar sign, by raising his thumb to his forehead, and drawing it twice across his brow. Then he remained impassible. This had passed so rapidly, that when M. de Gernande turned round, Rodin was at a distance of several steps from Dr. Baleinier, and looking at Mdlle. de Cardoville with respectful interest.

"Permit me to accompany you, sir," said the doctor, preceding the magistrate, whom Mdlle. de Cardoville saluted with much affability. Then both went out, and Rodin remained alone with the young lady.

After conducting M. de Gernande to the outer door of the house, M. Baleinier made haste to read the pencil-note written by Rodin; it ran as follows: "The magistrate is going to the convent, by way of the street. Run round by the garden, and tell the Superior to obey the order I have given with regard to the two young girls. It is of the utmost importance."

The peculiar sign which Rodin had made, and the tenor of this note, proved to Dr. Baleinier, who was passing from surprise to amazement, that the secretary, far from betraying the reverend father, was still acting for the Greater Glory of the Lord. However, whilst he obeyed the orders, M. Baleinier sought in vain to penetrate the motives of Rodin's inexplicable conduct, who had himself informed the authorities of an affair that was to have been hushed up, and that might have the most disastrous consequences for Father d'Aigrigny, Madame de Saint-Dizier, and Baleinier himself. But let us return to Rodin, left alone with Mdlle, de Cardoville.

CHAPTER XXXIV.

FATHER D'AIGRIGNY'S SECRETARY.

Hardly had the magistrate and Dr. Baleinier disappeared, than Mdlle. de Cardoville, whose countenance was beaming with joy, exclaimed, as she looked at Rodin with a mixture of respect and gratitude, "At length, thanks to you, sir, I am free—free! Oh, I had never before felt how much happiness, expansion, delight, there is in that adorable word—liberty!"

Her bosom rose and fell, her rosy nostrils dilated, her vermilion lips were half open, as if she again inhaled with rapture pure and vivifying air.

"I have been only a few days in this horrible place," she resumed, "but I have suffered enough from my captivity to make me resolve never to let a year pass without restoring to liberty some poor prisoners for debt. This vow no doubt appears to belong a little to the Middle Ages," added she, with a smile; "but I would fain borrow from that noble epoch something more than its old windows and furniture. So, doubly thanks, sir!—for I take you as a partner in that project of deliverance, which has just (you see) unfolded itself in the midst of the happiness I owe to you, and by which you seem so much affected. Oh! let my joy speak my gratitude, and pay you for your generous aid!" exclaimed the young girl with enthusiasm.

Mdlle. de Cardoville had truly remarked a complete transfiguration in the countenance of Rodin. This man, lately so harsh, severe, inflexible, with regard to Dr. Baleinier, appeared now under the influence of the mildest and most tender sentiments. His little, half-veiled eyes were fixed upon Adrienne with an expression of ineffable interest. Then, as if he wished to tear himself from these impressions, he said, speaking to himself, "Come, come, no weakness. Time is too precious; my mission is not fulfilled. My dear young lady," added he, addressing himself to Adrienne, "believe what I say—we will talk hereafter of gratitude—but we have now to talk of the present so important for you and your family. Do you know what is taking place?"

Adrienne looked at the Jesuit with surprise, and said, "What is taking place, sir?"

"Do you know the real motive of your imprisonment in this house? Do you know what influenced the Princess de Saint-Dizier and Abbe d'Aigrigny?"

At the sound of those detested names, Mdlle. de Cardoville's face, now so full of happiness, became suddenly sad, and she answered with bitterness,

"It is hatred, sir, that no doubt animated Madame de Saint-Dizier against me."

"Yes, hatred; and, moreover, the desire to rob you with impunity of an immense fortune."

"Me, sir! how?"

"You must be ignorant, my dear young lady, of the interest you had to be in the Rue Saint-Francois on the 13th February, for an inheritance?"

"I was ignorant, sir, of the date and details: but I knew by some family papers, and thanks to an extraordinary circumstance, that one of our ancestors—"

"Had left an enormous sum to be divided between his descendants; is it not so?"

"Yes, sir."

"But what unfortunately you did not know, my dear young lady, was that the heirs were all bound to be present at a certain hour on the 13th February. This day and hour once past, the absent would forfeit their claim. Do you now understand why you have been imprisoned here, my dear young lady?"

"Yes, yes; I understand it," cried Mdlle. de Cardoville; "cupidity was added to the hatred which my aunt felt for me. All is explained. Marshal Simon's daughters, having the same right as I had have, like me, been imprisoned."

"And yet," cried Rodin, "you and they were not the only victims."

"Who, then, are the others, sir?"

"A young East Indian."

"Prince Djalma?" said Adrienne, hastily.

"For the same reason he has been nearly poisoned with a narcotic."

"Great God!" cried the young girl, clasping her hands in horror. "It is fearful. That young prince, who was said to have so noble and generous a character! But I had sent to Cardoville Castle—"

"A confidential person, to fetch the prince to Paris—I know it, my dear young lady; but, by means of a trick, your friend was got out of the way, and the young Oriental delivered to his enemies."

"And where is he now?"

"I have only vague information on the subject. I know that he is in Paris, and do not despair of finding him. I shall pursue my researches with an almost paternal ardor, for we cannot too much love the rare qualities of that poor king's son. What a heart, my dear young lady! what a heart! Oh, it is a heart of gold, pure and bright as the gold of his country!"

"We must find the prince, sir," said Adrienne with emotion; "let me entreat you to neglect nothing for that end. He is my relation—alone here—without support—without assistance."

"Certainly," replied Rodin, with commiseration. "Poor boy!—for he is almost a boy—eighteen or nineteen years of age—thrown into the heart of Paris, of this hell—with his fresh, ardent, half-savage passions—with his simplicity and confidence—to what perils may he not be exposed?"

"Well, we must first find him, sir," said Adrienne, hastily; "and then we will save him from these dangers. Before I was confined here, I learned his arrival in France, and sent a confidential person to offer him the services of an unknown friend. I now see that this mad idea, with which I have been so much reproached, was a very sensible one. I am more convinced of it than ever. The prince belongs to my family, and I owe him a generous hospitality. I had destined for him the lodge I occupied at my aunt's."

"And you, my dear young lady?"

"To-day, I shall remove to a house, which I had prepared some time ago, with the determination of quitting Madame de Saint-Dizier, and living alone as I pleased. Then, sir, as you seem bent upon being the good genius of our family, be as generous with regard to Prince Djalma, as you have been to me and Marshal Simon's daughters. I entreat you to discover the hiding-place of this poor king's son, as you call him; keep my secret for me, and conduct him to the house offered by the unknown friend. Let him not disquiet himself about anything; all his wants shall be provided for; he shall live—like a prince."

"Yes; he will indeed live like a prince, thanks to your royal munificence. But never was such kind interest better deserved. It is enough to see (as I have seen) his fine, melancholy countenance—"

"You have seen him, then, sir?" said Adrienne, interrupting Rodin.

"Yes, my dear young lady; I was with him for about two hours. It was quite enough to judge of him. His charming features are the mirror of his soul."

"And where did you see him, sir?"

"At your old Chateau de Cardoville, my dear young lady, near which he had been shipwrecked in a storm, and whither I had gone to—" Rodin hesitated for a moment, and then, as if yielding to the frankness of his disposition, added: "Whither I had gone to commit a bad action—a shameful, miserable action, I must confess!"

"You, sir?—at Cardoville House—to commit a bad action?" cried Adrienne, much surprised.

"Alas! yes, my dear young lady," answered Rodin with simplicity. "In one word, I had orders from Abbe d'Aigrigny, to place your former bailiff in the alternative either of losing his situation or lending himself to a mean action—something, in fact, that resembled spying and calumny; but the honest, worthy man refused."

"Why, who are you, sir?" said Mdlle. de Cardoville, more and more astonished.

"I am Rodin, lately secretary of the Abbe d'Aigrigny—a person of very little importance, as you see."

It is impossible to describe the accent, at once humble and ingenuous, of the Jesuit, as he pronounced these words, which he accompanied with a respectful bow. On this revelation, Mdlle. de Cardoville drew back abruptly. We have said that Adrienne had sometimes heard talk of Rodin, the humble secretary of the Abbe d'Aigrigny, as a sort of obedient and passive machine. That was not all; the bailiff of Cardoville Manor, writing to Adrienne on the subject of Prince Djalma, had complained of the perfidious and dishonest propositions of Rodin. She felt, therefore, a vague suspicion, when she heard that her liberator was the man who had played so odious a part. Yet this unfavorable feeling was balanced by the sense of what she owed to Rodin, and by his frank denunciation of Abbe d'Aigrigny before the magistrate. And then the Jesuit, by his own confession, had anticipated, as it were, the reproaches that might have been addressed to him. Still, it was with a kind of cold reserve that Mdlle. de Cardoville resumed this dialogue, which she had commenced with as much frankness as warmth and sympathy.

Rodin perceived the impression he had made. He expected it. He was not the least disconcerted when Mdlle. de Cardoville said to him, as she fixed upon him a piercing glance, "Ah! you are M. Rodin—secretary to the Abbe d'Aigrigny?"

"Say ex-secretary, if you please, my dear young lady," answered the Jesuit; "for you see clearly that I can never again enter the house of the Abbe d'Aigrigny. I have made of him an implacable enemy, and I am now without employment—but no matter—nay, so much the better—since, at this price, the wicked are unmasked, and honest people rescued."

These words, spoken with much simplicity, and dignity, revived a feeling of pity in Adrienne's heart. She thought within herself that, after all, the poor old man spoke the truth. Abbe d'Aigrigny's hate, after this exposure, would be inexorable, and Rodin had braved it for the sake of a generous action.

Still Mdlle. de Cardoville answered coldly, "Since you knew, sir, that the propositions you were charged to make to the bailiff of Cardoville were shameful and perfidious, how could you undertake the mission?"

"How?" replied Rodin, with a sort of painful impatience; "why, because I was completely under Abbe d'Aigrigny's charm, one of the most prodigiously clever men I have ever known, and, as I only discovered the day before yesterday, one of the most prodigiously dangerous men there is in the world. He had conquered my scruples, by persuading me that the End justifies the Means. I must confess that the end he seemed to propose to himself was great and beautiful; but the day before yesterday I was cruelly undeceived. I was awakened, as it were, by a thunder-peal. Oh, my dear young lady!" added Rodin, with a sort of embarrassment and confusion, "let us talk no more of my fatal journey to Cardoville. Though I was only an ignorant and blind instrument, I feel as ashamed and grieved at it as if I had acted for myself. It weighs upon me, it oppresses me. I entreat you, let us speak rather of yourself, and of what interests you—for the soul expands with generous thoughts, even as the breast is dilated in pure and healthful air."

Rodin had confessed his fault so spontaneously, he explained it so naturally, he appeared to regret it so sincerely, that Adrienne, whose suspicions had no other grounds, felt her distrust a good deal diminished.

"So," she resumed, still looking attentively at Rodin, "it was at Cardoville that you saw Prince Djalma?"

"Yes, madame; and my affection for him dates from that interview. Therefore I will accomplish my task. Be satisfied, my dear young lady; like you, like Marshal Simon's daughters, the prince shall avoid being the victim of this detestable plot, which unhappily does not stop there."

"And who besides, then, is threatened?"

"M. Hardy, a man full of honor and probity, who is also your relation, and interested in this inheritance, but kept away from Paris by infamous treachery. And another heir, an unfortunate artisan, who falling into a trap cleverly baited, has been thrown into a prison for debt."

"But, sir," said Adrienne, suddenly, "for whose advantage was this abominable plot, which really alarms me, first devised?"

"For the advantage of Abbe d'Aigrigny," answered Rodin.

"How, and by what right! Was he also an heir?"

"It would take too long to explain it to you, my dear young lady. You will know all one day. Only be convinced that your family has no more bitter enemy that Abbe d'Aigrigny."

"Sir," said Adrienne, giving way to one last suspicion, "I will speak frankly to you. How can I have deserved the interest that you seem to take in me, and that you even extend to all the members of my family?"

"My dear young lady," answered Rodin, with a smile, "were I to tell you the cause, you would only laugh at, or misapprehend me."

"Speak, I beg of you, sir. Do not mistrust me or yourself."

"Well, then, I became interested in you—devoted to you—because your heart is generous, your mind lofty, your character independent and proud. Once attached to you, those of your race, who are indeed themselves worthy of interest, were no longer indifferent to me. To serve them was to serve you also."

"But, sir—admitting that you suppose me worthy of the too flattering praises you bestow upon me—how could you judge of my heart, my mind, my character?"

"I will tell you, my dear young lady; but first I must make another confession, that fills me with shame. If you were not even so wonderfully endowed, what you have suffered in this house should suffice to command the interest of every honest man—don't you think so?"

"I do think it should, sir."

"I might thus explain the interest I feel in you. But no—I confess it—that would not have sufficed with me. Had you been only Mdlle. de Cardoville—a rich, noble, beautiful young lady—I should doubtless have pitied your misfortune; but I should have said to myself, 'This poor young lady is certainly much to be pitied; but what can I, poor man, do in it? My only resource is my post of secretary to the Abbe d'Aigrigny, and he would be the first that must be attacked. He is all-powerful, and I am nothing. To engage in a struggle with him would be to ruin myself, without the hope of saving this unfortunate person.' But when I learnt what you were, my dear young lady, I revolted, in spite of my inferiority. 'No,' I said, 'a thousand times, no! So fine an intellect, so great a heart, shall not be the victims of an abominable plot. I may perish in the struggle, but I will at least make the attempt.'"

No words can paint the mixture of delicacy, energy, and sensibility with which Rodin uttered these sentiments. As it often happens with people singularly repulsive and ill-favored, if they can once bring you to forget their ugliness, their very deformity becomes a source of interest and commiseration, and you say to yourself, "What a pity that such a mind, such a soul, should inhabit so poor a body!"—and you are touched and softened by the contrast.

It was thus that Mdlle. de Cardoville began to look upon Rodin. He had shown himself as simple and affectionate towards her as he had been brutal and insolent to Dr. Baleinier. One thing only excited the lively curiosity of Mdlle. de Cardoville—she wished to know how Rodin had conceived the devotion and admiration which she seemed to inspire.

"Forgive my indiscreet and obstinate curiosity, sir, but I wish to know—"

"How you were morally revealed to me—is it not so? Oh, my dear young lady! nothing is more simple. I will explain it to you in two words. The Abbe d'Aigrigny saw in me nothing but a writing-machine, an obtuse, mute, blind instrument—"

"I thought M. d'Aigrigny had more penetration."

"And you are right, my dear young lady; he is a man of unparalleled sagacity; but I deceived him by affecting more than simplicity. Do not, therefore, think me false. No; I am proud in my manner—and my pride consists in never appearing above my position, however subaltern it may be! Do you know why? It is that, however haughty may be my superiors, I can say to myself, 'They do not know my value. It is the inferiority of my condition, not me, that they humiliate.' By this I gain doubly—my self-love is spared, and I hate no one."

"Yes, I understand that sort of pride," said Adrienne, more and more struck with Rodin's original turn of mind.

"But let us return to what concerns you, my dear young lady. On the eve of the 13th of February, the Abbe d'Aigrigny delivered to me a paper in shorthand, and said to me, 'Transcribe this examination; you may add that it is to support the decision of a family council, which has declared, in accordance with the report of Dr. Baleinier, the state of mind of Mdlle. de Cardoville to be sufficiently alarming to render it necessary to confine her in a lunatic asylum.'"

"Yes," said Adrienne, with bitterness; "it related to a long interview, which I had with the Princess de Saint-Dizier, my aunt, and which was taken down without my knowledge."

"Behold me, then, poring over my shorthand report, and beginning to transcribe it. At the end of the first ten lines, I was struck with stupor. I knew not if I were awake or dreaming. 'What! mad?' They must be themselves insane who dare assert so monstrous a proposition!—More and more interested, I continued my reading—I finished it—Oh! then, what shall I say? What I felt, my dear young lady, it is impossible to express. It was sympathy, delight, enthusiasm!"

"Sir," said Adrienne.

"Yes, my dear young lady, enthusiasm! Let not the words shock your modesty. Know that these ideas, so new, so independent, so courageous which you expressed to your aunt with so much brilliancy, are, without your being aware of it, common to you and another person, for whom you will one day feel the most tender and religious respect."

"Of whom do you speak, sir?" cried Mdlle. de Cardoville, more and more interested.

After a moment's apparent hesitation, Rodin resumed, "No, no—it is useless now to inform you of it. All I can tell you, my dear young lady, is that, when I had finished my reading, I ran to Abbe d'Aigrigny's, to convince him of the error into which he had fallen with regard to you. It was impossible then to find him; but yesterday morning I told him plainly what I thought. He only appeared surprised to find that I could think at all. He received my communications with contemptuous silence. I thought him deceived; I continued my remonstrances, but quite in vain. He ordered me to follow him to the house, where the testament of your ancestor was to be opened. I was so blind with regard to the Abbe d'Aigrigny, that it required the successive arrivals of the soldier, of his son, and of Marshal Simon's father, to open my eyes thoroughly. Their indignation unveiled to me the extent of a conspiracy, plotted long ago, and carried on with terrible ability. Then, I understood why you were confined here as a lunatic; why the daughters of Marshal Simon were imprisoned in a convent. Then a thousand recollections returned to my mind; fragments of letters and statements, which had been given me to copy or decipher, and of which I had never been able to find the explanation, put me on the track of this odious machination. To express then and there the sudden horror I felt at these crimes, would have been to ruin all. I did not make this mistake. I opposed cunning to cunning; I appeared even more eager than Abbe d'Aigrigny. Had this immense inheritance been destined for me alone, I could not have shown myself more grasping and merciless. Thanks to this stratagem, Abbe d'Aigrigny had no suspicion. A providential accident having rescued the inheritance from his hands, he left the house in a state of profound consternation. For my part, I felt indescribable joy; for I had now the means of saving and avenging you, my dear young lady. As usual, I went yesterday evening to my place of business. During the absence of the abbe, it was easy for me to peruse the correspondence relative to the inheritance. In this way I was able to unite all the threads of this immense plot. Oh! then, my dear young lady, I remained, struck with horror, in presence of the discoveries that I made, and that I never should have made under any other circumstances."

"What discoveries, sir?"

"There are some secrets which are terrible to those who possess them. Do not ask me to explain, my dear young lady; but, in this examination, the league formed against you and your relations, from motives of insatiable cupidity, appeared to me in all its dark audacity. Thereupon, the lively and deep interest which I already felt for you, my dear young lady, was augmented greatly, and extended itself to the other innocent victims of this infernal conspiracy. In spite of my weakness, I determined to risk all, to unmask the Abbe d'Aigrigny. I collected the necessary proofs, to give my declaration before the magistrate the needful authority; and, this morning, I left the abbe's house without revealing to him my projects. He might have employed some violent method to detain me; yet it would have been cowardly to attack him without warning. Once out of his house, I wrote to him, that I had in my hands proof enough of his crimes, to attack him openly in the face of day. I would accuse, and he must defend himself. I went directly to a magistrate, and you know the rest."

At this juncture, the door opened, and one of the nurses appeared, and said to Rodin: "Sir, the messenger that you and the magistrate sent to the Rue Brise-Miche has just come back."

"Has he left the letter?"

"Yes, sir; and it was taken upstairs directly."

"Very well. Leave us!" The nurse went out.

CHAPTER XXXV.

SYMPATHY.

If it had been possible for Mdlle. de Cardoville to harbor any suspicion of the sincerity of Rodin's devotion, it must have given way before this reasoning, unfortunately so simple and undeniable. How could she suppose the faintest complicity between the Abbe d'Aigrigny and his secretary, when it was the latter who completely unveiled the machinations of his master, and exposed them to the tribunals? when in this, Rodin went even further than Mdlle. de Cardoville would herself have gone? Of what secret design could she suspect the Jesuit? At worst, of a desire to earn by his services the profitable patronage of the young lady.

And then, had he not just now protested against this supposition, by declaring his devotion, not to Mdlle. de Cardoville—not to the fair, rich, noble lady—but to the high-souled and generous girl? Finally, as Rodin had said himself, could any but a miserable wretch fail to be interested in Adrienne's fate? A strange mixture of curiosity, surprise, and interest, was joined with Mdlle. de Cardoville's feelings of gratitude towards Rodin. Yet, as she recognized the superior mind under that humble exterior, she was suddenly struck with a grave suspicion. "Sir," said she to Rodin, "I always confess to the persons I esteem the doubts they may have inspired, so that they may justify themselves, and excuse me, if I am wrong."

Rodin looked at Mdlle. de Cardoville with surprise, as if mentally calculating the suspicions than she might entertain, and replied, after a moment's silence: "You are perhaps thinking of my journey to Cardoville, of my base proposals to your good and worthy bailiff? Oh! if you—"

"No, no, sir," said Adrienne, interrupting him; "you made that confession spontaneously, and I quite understand, that, blinded with regard to M. d'Aigrigny, you passively executed instructions repugnant to your delicacy. But how comes it, that, with your incontestable merits, you have so long occupied so mean a position in his service?"

"It is true," said Rodin, with a smile; "that must impress you unfavorably, my dear young lady; for a man of any capacity, who remains long in an inferior condition, has evidently some radical vice, some bad or base passion—"

"It is generally true, sir."

"And personally true—with regard to myself."

"What, sir! do you make this avowal?"

"Alas! I confess that I have a bad passion, to which, for forty years, I have sacrificed all chances of attaining to a better position."

"And this passion, sir?"

"Since I must make the unpleasant avowal, this passion is indolence—yes, indolence—the horror of all activity of mind, of all moral responsibility, of taking the lead in anything. With the twelve hundred francs that Abbe d'Aigrigny gave me, I was the happiest man in the world; I trusted to the nobleness of his views; his thoughts became mine, his wishes mine. My work once finished, I returned to my poor little chamber, I lighted my fire, I dined on vegetables—then, taking up some book of philosophy, little known, and dreaming over it, I gave free course to my imagination, which, restrained all the day long, carried me through numberless theories to a delicious Utopia. Then, from the eminences of my intelligence, lifted up Lord knows whither, by the audacity of my thoughts, I seemed to look down upon my master, and upon the great men of the earth. This fever lasted for three or four hours, after which I had a good sleep; and, the next morning, I went lightly to my work, secure of my daily bread, without cares for the future, living content with little, waiting with impatience for the delights of my solitary evening, and saying to myself as I went on writing like a stupid machine: 'And yet—and yet—if I chose!'—"

"Doubtless, you could, like others, surer than others, have reached a higher position," said Adrienne, greatly struck with Rodin's practical philosophy.

"Yes, I think I could have done so; but for what purpose?—You see, my dear young lady, what often renders people of some merit puzzles to the vulgar, is that they are frequently content to say: 'If I chose!'"

"But, sir, without attaching much importance to the luxuries of life, there is a certain degree of comfort, which age renders almost indispensable, and which you seem to have utterly renounced."

"Undeceive yourself, if you please, my dear young lady," said Rodin, with a playful smile. "I am a true Sybarite; I require absolutely warm clothes, a good stove, a soft mattress, a good piece of bread, a fresh radish, flavored with good cheap salt, and some good, clear water; and, notwithstanding this complication of wants, my twelve hundred francs have always more than sufficed, for I have been able to make some little savings."

"But now that you are without employment, how will you manage to live, sir?" said Adrienne, more and more interested by the singularities of this man, and wishing to put his disinterestedness to the proof.

"I have laid by a little, which will serve me till I have unravelled the last thread of Father d'Aigrigny's dark designs. I owe myself this reparation, for having been his dupe; three or four days, I hope, will complete the work. After that, I have the certainty of meeting with a situation, in my native province, under a collector of taxes: some time ago, the offer was made me by a friend; but then I would not leave Father d'Aigrigny, notwithstanding the advantages proposed. Fancy, my dear young lady—eight hundred francs, with board and lodging! As I am a little of the roughest, I should have preferred lodging apart; but, as they give me so much, I must submit to this little inconvenience."

Nothing could exceed Rodin's ingenuity, in making these little household confidences (so abominably false) to Mdlle. de Cardoville, who felt her last suspicions give way.

"What, sir?" said she to the Jesuit, with interest; "in three or four days, you mean to quit Paris?"

"I hope to do so, my dear young lady; and that," added he, in a mysterious tone, "and that for many reasons. But what would be very precious to me," he resumed, in a serious voice, as he looked at Adrienne with emotion, "would be to carry with me the conviction, that you did me the justice to believe, that, on merely reading your interview with the Princess de Saint-Dizier, I recognized at once qualities quite unexampled in our day, in a young person of your age and condition."

"Ah, sir!" said Adrienne, with a smile, "do not think yourself obliged to return so soon the sincere praises that I bestowed on your superiority of mind. I should be better pleased with ingratitude."

"Oh, no! I do not flatter you, my dear young lady. Why should I? We may probably never meet again. I do not flatter you; I understand you—that's all—and what will seem strange to you, is, that your appearance complete, the idea which I had already formed of you, my dear young lady, in reading your interview with your aunt: and some parts of your character, hitherto obscure to me, are now fully displayed."

"Really, sir, you astonish me more and more."

"I can't help it! I merely describe my impressions. I can now explain perfectly, for example, your passionate love of the beautiful, your eager worship of the refinements of the senses, your ardent aspirations for a better state of things, your courageous contempt of many degrading and servile customs, to which woman is condemned; yes, now I understand the noble pride with which you contemplate the mob of vain, self-sufficient, ridiculous men, who look upon woman as a creature destined for their service, according to the laws made after their own not very handsome image. In the eyes of these hedge-tyrants, woman, a kind of inferior being to whom a council of cardinals deigned to grant a soul by a majority of two voices, ought to think herself supremely happy in being the servant of these petty pachas, old at thirty, worn-out, used up, weary with excesses, wishing only for repose, and seeking, as they say, to make an end of it, which they set about by marrying some poor girl, who is on her side desirous to make a beginning."

Mdlle. de Cardoville would certainly have smiled at these satirical remarks, if she had not been greatly struck by hearing Rodin express in such appropriate terms her own ideas, though it was the first time in her life that she saw this dangerous man. Adrienne forgot, or rather, she was not aware, that she had to deal with a Jesuit of rare intelligence, uniting the information and the mysterious resources of the police-spy with the profound sagacity of the confessor; one of those diabolic priests, who, by the help of a few hints, avowals, letters, reconstruct a character, as Cuvier could reconstruct a body from zoological fragments. Far from interrupting Rodin, Adrienne listened to him with growing curiosity. Sure of the effect he produced, he continued, in a tone of indignation: "And your aunt and the Abbe d'Aigrigny treated you as mad, because you revolted against the yoke of such tyrants! because, hating the shameful vices of slavery, you chose to be independent with the suitable qualities of independence, free with the proud virtues of liberty!"

"But, sir," said Adrienne, more and more surprised, "how can my thoughts be so familiar to you?"

"First, I know you perfectly, thanks to your interview with the Princess de Saint-Dizier: and next, if it should happen that we both pursue the same end, though by different means," resumed Rodin, artfully, as he looked at Mdlle. de Cardoville with an air of intelligence, "why should not our convictions be the same?"

"I do not understand you, sir. Of what end do you speak?"

"The end pursued incessantly by all lofty, generous, independent spirits—some acting, like you, my dear young lady, from passion, from instinct, without perhaps explaining to themselves the high mission they are called on to ful, fil. Thus, for example, when you take pleasure in the most refined delights, when you surround yourself with all that charms the senses, do you think that you only yield to the attractions of the beautiful, to the desire of exquisite enjoyments? No! ah, no! for then you would be incomplete, odiously selfish, a dry egotist, with a fine taste—nothing more—and at your age, it would be hideous, my dear young lady, it would be hideous!"

"And do you really think thus severely of me?" said Adrienne, with uneasiness, so much influence had this man irresistibly attained over her.

"Certainly, I should think thus of you, if you loved luxury for luxury's sake; but, no—quite another sentiment animates you," resumed the Jesuit. "Let us reason a little. Feeling a passionate desire for all these enjoyments, you know their value and their need more than any one—is it not so?"

"It is so," replied Adrienne, deeply interested.

"Your gratitude and favor are then necessarily acquired by those who, poor, laborious, and unknown, have procured for you these marvels of luxury, which you could not do without?"

"This feeling of gratitude is so strong in me, sir," replied Adrienne, more and more pleased to find herself so well understood, "that I once had inscribed on a masterpiece of goldsmith's work, instead of the name of the seller, that of the poor unknown artist who designed it, and who has since risen to his true place."

"There you see, I was not deceived," went on Rodin; "the taste for enjoyment renders you grateful to those who procure it for you; and that is not all; here am I, an example, neither better nor worse than my neighbors, but accustomed to privations, which cause me no suffering—so that the privations of others necessarily touch me less nearly than they do you, my dear young lady; for your habits of comfort must needs render you more compassionate towards misfortune. You would yourself suffer too much from poverty, not to pity and succor those who are its victims."

"Really, sir," said Adrienne, who began to feel herself under the fatal charm of Rodin, "the more I listen to you, the more I am convinced that you would defend a thousand times better than I could those ideas for which I was so harshly reproached by Madame de Saint-Dizier and Abbe d'Aigrigny. Oh! speak, speak, sir! I cannot tell you with what happiness, with what pride I listen."

Attentive and moved, her eyes fixed on the Jesuit with as much interest as sympathy and curiosity, Adrienne, by a graceful toss of the head that was habitual to her, threw hack her long, golden curls, the better to contemplate Rodin, who thus resumed: "You are astonished, my dear young lady, that you were not understood by your aunt or by Abbe d'Aigrigny! What point of contact had you with these hypocritical, jealous, crafty minds, such as I can judge them to be now? Do you wish a new proof of their hateful blindness? Among what they called your monstrous follies, which was the worst, the most damnable? Why, your resolution to live alone and in your own way, to dispose freely of the present and the future. They declared this to be odious, detestable, immoral. And yet—was this resolution dictated by a mad love of liberty? no!—by a disordered aversion to all restraint? no!—by the desire of singularity?—no!—for then I, too, should have blamed you severely."

"Other reasons have indeed guided me, sir, I assure you," said Adrienne eagerly, for she had become very eager for the esteem with which her character might inspire Rodin.

"Oh! I know it well; your motives could only be excellent ones," replied the Jesuit. "Why then did you take this resolution, so much called in question? Was it to brave established etiquette? no! for you respected them until the hate of Mme. de Saint-Dizier forced you to withdraw yourself from her unbearable guardianship. Was it to live alone, to escape the eyes of the world? no! you would be a hundred times more open to observation in this than any other condition. Was it to make a bad use of your liberty? no, ah, no! those who design evil seek for darkness and solitude; while you place yourself right before the jealous anal envious eyes of the vulgar crowd. Why then do you take this determination, so courageous and rare, unexampled in a young person of your age? Shall I tell you, my dear young lady? It is, that you wish to prove, by your example, that a woman of pure heart and honest mind, with a firm character and independence of soul, may nobly and proudly throw off the humiliating guardianship that custom has imposed upon her. Yes, instead of accepting the fate of a revolted slave, a life only destined to hypocrisy or vice, you wish to live freely in presence of all the world, independent, honorable, and respected. You wish to have, like man, the exercise of your own free will, the entire responsibility of all your actions, so as to establish the fact, that a woman left completely to herself, may equal man in reason, wisdom, uprightness, and surpass him indelicacy and dignity. That is your design, my dear young lady. It is noble and great. Will your example be imitated? I hope it may; but whether it be so or not, your generous attempt, believe me, will place you in a high and worthy position."

Mdlle. de Cardoville's eyes shone with a proud and gentle brightness, her cheeks were slightly colored, her bosom heaved, she raised her charming head with a movement of involuntary pride; at length completely under the charm of that diabolical man she exclaimed: "But, sir, who are you that can thus know and analyze my most secret thoughts, and read my soul more clearly than myself, so as to give new life and action to those ideas of independence which have long stirred within me? Who are you, that can thus elevate me in my own eyes, for now I am conscious of accomplishing a mission, honorable to myself, and perhaps useful to my sisters immersed in slavery? Once again, sir, who are you?"

"Who am I, madame?" answered Rodin, with a smile of the greatest good nature; "I have already told you that I am a poor old man, who for the last forty years, having served in the day time as a writing machine to record the ideas of others, went home every evening to work out ideas of his own—a good kind of man who, from his garret, watches and even takes some little share in the movement of generous spirits, advancing towards an end that is nearer than is commonly thought. And thus, my dear young lady, as I told you just now, you and I are both tending towards the same objects, though you may do the same without reflection, and merely in obedience to your rare and divine instincts. So continue so to live, fair, free, and happy!—it is your mission—more providential than you may think it. Yes; continue to surround yourself with all the marvels of luxury and art; refine your senses, purify your tastes, by the exquisite choice of your enjoyments; by genius, grace, and purity raise yourself above the stupid and ill-favored mob of men, that will instantly surround you, when they behold you alone and free; they will consider you an easy prey, destined to please their cupidity, their egotism, their folly.

"Laugh at them, and mock these idiotic and sordid pretensions. Be the queen of your own world, and make yourself respected as a queen. Love—shine—enjoy—it is your part upon earth. All the flowers, with which you are whelmed in profusion, will one day bear fruit. You think that you have lived only for pleasure; in reality, you will have lived for the noblest aims that could tempt a great and lofty soul. And so—some years hence—we may meet again, perhaps; you, fairer and more followed than ever; I, older and more obscure. But, no matter—a secret voice, I am sure, says to you at this moment, that between us two, however different, there exists an invisible bond, a mysterious communion, which nothing hereafter will ever be able to destroy!"

He uttered these final words in a tone of such profound emotion, that Adrienne started. Rodin had approached without her perceiving it, and without, as it were, walking at all, for he dragged his steps along the floor, with a sort of serpent motion; and he had spoken with so much warmth and enthusiasm, that his pale face had become slightly tinged, and his repulsive ugliness had almost disappeared before the brilliancy of his small sharp eyes, now wide open, and fixed full upon Adrienne. The latter leaned forward, with half-open lips and deep-drawn breath, nor could she take her eyes from the Jesuit's; he had ceased to speak, and yet she was still listening. The feelings of the fair young lady, in presence of this little old man, dirty, ugly, and poor, were inexplicable. That comparison so common, and yet so true, of the frightful fascination of the bird by the serpent, might give some idea of the singular impression made upon her. Rodin's tactics were skillful and sure. Until now, Mdlle. de Cardoville had never analyzed her tastes or instincts. She had followed them, because they were inoffensive and charming. How happy and proud she then was sure to be to hear a man of superior mind not only praise these tendencies, for which she had been heretofore so severely blamed, but congratulate her upon them, as upon something great, noble, and divine! If Rodin had only addressed himself to Adrienne's self-conceit, he would have failed in his perfidious designs, for she had not the least spark of vanity. But he addressed himself to all that was enthusiastic and generous in her heart; that which he appeared to encourage and admire in her was really worthy of encouragement and admiration. How could she fail to be the dupe of such language, concealing though it did such dark and fatal projects?

Struck with the Jesuit's rare intelligence, feeling her curiosity greatly excited by some mysterious words that he had purposely uttered, hardly explaining to herself the strange influence which this pernicious counsellor already exercised over her, and animated by respectful compassion for a man of his age and talents placed in so precarious a position, Adrienne said to him, with all her natural cordiality, "A man of your merit and character, sir, ought not to be at the mercy of the caprice of circumstances. Some of your words have opened a new horizon before me; I feel that, on many points, your counsels may be of the greatest use to me. Moreover, in coming to fetch me from this house, and in devoting yourself to the service of other persons of my family, you have shown me marks of interest which I cannot forget without ingratitude. You have lost a humble but secure situation. Permit me—"

"Not a word more, my dear young lady," said Rodin, interrupting Mdlle. de Cardoville, with an air of chagrin. "I feel for you the deepest sympathy; I am honored by having ideas in common with you; I believe firmly that some day you will have to ask advice of the poor old philosopher; and, precisely because of all that, I must and ought to maintain towards you the most complete independence."

"But, sir, it is I that would be the obliged party, if you deigned to accept what I offer."

"Oh, my dear young lady," said Rodin, with a smile: "I know that your generosity would always know how to make gratitude light and easy; but, once more, I cannot accept anything from you. One day, perhaps, you will know why."

"One day?"

"It is impossible for me to tell you more. And then, supposing I were under an obligation to you, how could I tell you all that was good and beautiful in your actions? Hereafter, if you are somewhat indebted to me for my advice, so much the better; I shall be the more ready to blame you, if I find anything to blame."

"In this way, sir, you would forbid me to be grateful to you."

"No, no," said Rodin, with apparent emotion. "Oh, believe me! there will come a solemn moment, in which you may repay all, in a manner worthy of yourself and me."

This conversation was here interrupted by the nurse, who said to Adrienne as she entered: "Madame, there is a little humpback workwoman downstairs, who wishes to speak to you. As, according to the doctor's new orders, you are to do as you like, I have come to ask, if I am to bring her up to you. She is so badly dressed, that I did not venture."

"Bring her up, by all means," said Adrienne, hastily, for she had recognized Mother Bunch by the nurse's description. "Bring her up directly."

"The doctor has also left word, that his carriage is to be at your orders, madame; are the horses to be put to?"

"Yes, in a quarter of an hour," answered Adrienne to the nurse, who went out; then, addressing Rodin, she continued: "I do not think the magistrate can now be long, before he returns with Marshal Simon's daughters?"

"I think not, my dear young lady; but who is this deformed workwoman?" asked Rodin, with an air of indifference.

"The adopted sister of a gallant fellow, who risked all in endeavoring to rescue me from this house. And, sir," said Adrienne, with emotion, "this young workwoman is a rare and excellent creature. Never was a nobler mind, a more generous heart, concealed beneath an exterior less—"

But reflecting, that Rodin seemed to unite in his own person the same moral and physical contrasts as the sewing-girl, Adrienne stopped short, and then added, with inimitable grace, as she looked at the Jesuit, who was somewhat astonished at the sudden pause: "No; this noble girl is not the only person who proves how loftiness of soul, and superiority of mind, can make us indifferent to the vain advantages which belong only to the accidents of birth or fortune." At the moment of Adrienne speaking these last words, Mother Bunch entered the room.

CHAPTER XXXVI.

SUSPICIONS.

Mdlle. de Cardoville sprang hastily to meet the visitor, and said to her, in a voice of emotion, as she extended her arms towards her: "Come—come—there is no grating to separate us now!"

On this allusion, which reminded her how her poor, laborious hand had been respectfully kissed by the fair and rich patrician, the young workwoman felt a sentiment of gratitude, which was at once ineffable and proud. But, as she hesitated to respond to the cordial reception, Adrienne embraced her with touching affection. When Mother Bunch found herself clasped in the fair arms of Mdlle. de Cardoville, when she felt the fresh and rosy lips of the young lady fraternally pressed to her own pale and sickly cheek, she burst into tears without being able to utter a word. Rodin, retired in a corner of the chamber, locked on this scene with secret uneasiness. Informed of the refusal, so full of dignity, which Mother Bunch had opposed to the perfidious temptations of the superior of St. Mary's Convent, and knowing the deep devotion of this generous creature for Agricola—a devotion which for some days she had so bravely extended to Mdlle. de Cardoville—the Jesuit did not like to see the latter thus laboring to increase that affection. He thought, wisely, that one should never despise friend or enemy, however small they may appear. Now, devotion to Mdlle. de Cardoville constituted an enemy in his eyes; and we know, moreover, that Rodin combined in his character rare firmness, with a certain degree of superstitious weakness, and he now felt uneasy at the singular impression of fear which Mother Bunch inspired in him. He determined to recollect this presentiment.

Delicate natures sometimes display in the smallest things the most charming instincts of grace and goodness. Thus, when the sewing-girl was shedding abundant and sweet tears of gratitude, Adrienne took a richly embroidered handkerchief, and dried the pale and melancholy face. This action, so simple and spontaneous, spared the work-girl one humiliation; for, alas! humiliation and suffering are the two gulfs, along the edge of which misfortune continually passes. Therefore, the least kindness is in general a double benefit to the unfortunate. Perhaps the reader may smile in disdain at the puerile circumstance we mention. But poor Mother Bunch, not venturing to take from her pocket her old ragged handkerchief, would long have remained blinded by her tears, if Mdlle. de Cardoville had not come to her aid.

"Oh! you are so good—so nobly charitable, lady!" was all that the sempstress could say, in a tone of deep emotion; for she was still more touched by the attention of the young lady, than she would perhaps have been by a service rendered.

"Look there, sir," said Adrienne to Rodin, who drew near hastily. "Yes," added the young patrician, proudly, "I have indeed discovered a treasure. Look at her, sir; and love her as I love her, honor as I honor. She has one of those hearts for which we are seeking."

"And which, thank heaven, we are still able to find, my dear young lady!" said Rodin, as he bowed to the needle-woman.

The latter raised her eyes slowly, and looked at the Jesuit. At sight of that cadaverous countenance, which was smiling benignantly upon her, the young girl started. It was strange! she had never seen this man, and yet she felt instantly the same fear and repulsion that he had felt with regard to her. Generally timid and confused, the work-girl could not withdraw her eyes from Rodin's; her heart beat violently, as at the coming of some great danger, and, as the excellent creature feared only for those she loved, she approached Adrienne involuntarily, keeping her eyes fixed on Rodin. The Jesuit was too good a physiognomist not to perceive the formidable impression he had made, and he felt an increase of his instinctive aversion for the sempstress. Instead of casting down his eyes, he appeared to examine her with such sustained attention, that Mdlle. de Cardoville was astonished at it.

"I beg your pardon, my dear girl," said Rodin, as if recalling his recollections, and addressing himself to Mother Bunch, "I beg your pardon—but I think—if I am not deceived—did you not go a few days since to St. Mary's Convent, hard by?"

"Yes, sir."

"No doubt, it was you. Where then was my head?" cried Rodin. "It was you—I should have guessed it sooner."

"Of what do you speak, sir?" asked Adrienne.

"Oh! you are right, my dear young lady," said Rodin, pointing to the hunchback. "She has indeed a noble heart, such as we seek. If you knew with what dignity, with what courage this poor girl, who was out of work and, for her, to want work is to want everything—if you knew, I say, with what dignity she rejected the shameful wages that the superior of the convent was unprincipled enough to offer, on condition of her acting as a spy in a family where it was proposed to place her."

"Oh, that is infamous!" cried Mdlle. de Cardoville, with disgust. "Such a proposal to this poor girl—to her!"

"Madame," said Mother Bunch, bitterly, "I had no work, I was poor, they did not know me—and they thought they might propose anything to the likes of me."

"And I tell you," said Rodin, "that it was a double baseness on the part of the superior, to offer such temptation to misery, and it was doubly noble in you to refuse."

"Sir," said the sewing-girl, with modest embarrassment.

"Oh! I am not to be intimidated," resumed Rod in. "Praise or blame, I speak out roughly what I think. Ask this dear young lady," he added, with a glance at Adrienne. "I tell you plainly, that I think as well of you as she does herself."

"Believe me, dear," said Adrienne, "there are some sorts of praise which honor, recompense, and encourage; and M. Rodin's is of the number. I know it,—yes, I know it."

"Nay, my dear young lady, you must not ascribe to me all the honor of this judgment."

"How so, sir?"

"Is not this dear girl the adopted sister of Agricola Baudoin, the gallant workman, the energetic and popular poet? Is not the affection of such a man the best of guarantees, and does it not enable us to judge, as it were, by the label?" added Rodin, with a smile.

"You are right, sir," said Adrienne; "for, before knowing this dear girl, I began to feel deeply interested in her, from the day that her adopted brother spoke to me about her. He expressed himself with so much warmth, so much enthusiasm, that I at once conceived an esteem for the person capable of inspiring so noble an attachment."

These words of Adrienne, joined to another circumstance, had such an effect upon their hearer, that her pale face became crimson. The unfortunate hunchback loved Agricola, with love as passionate as it was secret and painful: the most indirect allusion to this fatal sentiment occasioned her the most cruel embarrassment. Now, the moment Mdlle. de Cardoville spoke of Agricola's attachment for Mother Bunch, the latter had encountered Rodin's observing and penetrating look fixed upon her. Alone with Adrienne, the sempstress would have felt only a momentary confusion on hearing the name of the smith; but unfortunately she fancied that the Jesuit, who already filled her with involuntary fear, had seen into her heart, and read the secrets of that fatal love, of which she was the victim. Thence the deep blushes of the poor girl, and the embarrassment so painfully visible, that Adrienne was struck with it.

A subtle and prompt mind, like Rodin's on perceiving the smallest effect, immediately seeks the cause. Proceeding by comparison, the Jesuit saw on one side a deformed, but intelligent young girl, capable of passionate devotion; on the other, a young workman, handsome, bold, frank, and full of talent. "Brought up together, sympathizing with each other on many points, there must be some fraternal affection between them," said he to himself; "but fraternal affection does not blush, and the hunchback blushed and grew troubled beneath my look; does she, then, Love Agricola?"

Once on the scent of this discovery, Rodin wished to pursue the investigation. Remarking the surprise and visible uneasiness that Mother Bunch had caused in Adrienne, he said to the latter, with a smile, looking significantly at the needlewoman: "You see, my dear young lady, how she blushes. The good girl is troubled by what we said of the attachment of this gallant workman."

The needlewoman hung down her head, overcome with confusion. After the pause of a second, during which Rodin preserved silence, so as to give time for his cruel remark to pierce the heart of the victim, the savage resumed: "Look at the dear girl! how embarrassed she appears!"

Again, after another silence, perceiving that Mother Bunch from crimson had become deadly pale, and was trembling in all her limbs, the Jesuit feared he had gone too far, whilst Adrienne said to her friend, with anxiety: "Why, dear child, are you so agitated?"

"Oh! it is clear enough," resumed Rodin, with an air of perfect simplicity; for having discovered what he wished to know, he now chose to appear unconscious. "It is quite clear and plain. This good girl has the modesty of a kind and tender sister for a brother. When you praise him, she fancies that she is herself praised."

"And she is as modest as she is excellent," added Adrienne, taking bath of the girl's hands, "the least praise, either of her adopted brother or of herself, troubles her in this way. But it is mere childishness, and I must scold her for it."

Mdlle. de Cardoville spoke sincerely, for the explanation given by Rodin appeared to her very plausible. Like all other persons who, dreading every moment the discovery of some painful secret have their courage as easily restored as shaken, Mother Bunch persuaded herself (and she needed to do so, to escape dying of shame), that the last words of Rodin were sincere, and that he had no idea of the love she felt for Agricola. So her agony diminished, and she found words to reply to Mdlle. de Cardoville.

"Excuse me, madame," she said timidly, "I am so little accustomed to such kindness as that with which you overwhelm me, that I make a sorry return for all your goodness."

"Kindness, my poor girl?" said Adrienne. "I have done nothing for you yet. But, thank heaven! from this day I shall be able to keep my promise, and reward your devotion to me, your courageous resignation, your sacred love of labor, and the dignity of which you have given so many proofs, under the most cruel privations. In a word, from this day, if you do not object to it, we will part no more."

"Madame, you are too kind," said Mother Bunch, in a trembling voice; "but I—"

"Oh! be satisfied," said Adrienne, anticipating her meaning. "If you accept my offer, I shall know how to reconcile with my desire (not a little selfish) of having you near me, the independence of your character, your habits of labor, your taste for retirement, and your anxiety to devote yourself to those who deserve commiseration; it is, I confess, by affording you the means of satisfying these generous tendencies, that I hope to seduce and keep you by me."

"But what have I done?" asked the other, simply, "to merit any gratitude from you? Did you not begin, on the contrary, by acting so generously to my adopted brother?"

"Oh! I do not speak of gratitude," said Adrienne; "we are quits. I speak of friendship and sincere affection, which I now offer you."

"Friendship to me, madame?"

"Come, come," said Adrienne, with a charming smile, "do not be proud because your position gives you the advantage. I have set my heart on having you for a friend, and you will see that it shall be so. But now that I think of it (a little late, you will say), what good wind brings you hither?"

"This morning M. Dagobert received a letter, in which he was requested to come to this place, to learn some news that would be of the greatest interest to him. Thinking it concerned Marshal Simon's daughters, he said to me: 'Mother Bunch, you have taken so much interest in those dear children, that you must come with me: you shall witness my joy on finding them, and that will be your reward.'"

Adrienne glanced at Rodin. The latter made an affirmative movement of the head, and answered: "Yes, yes, my dear young lady: it was I who wrote to the brave soldier, but without signing the letter, or giving any explanation. You shall know why."

"Then, my dear girl, why did you come alone?" said Adrienne.

"Alas, madame! on arriving here, it was your kind reception that made me forget my fears."

"What fears?" asked Rodin.

"Knowing that you lived here, madame, I supposed the letter was from you; I told M. Dagobert so, and he thought the same. When we arrived, his impatience was so great, that he asked at the door if the orphans were in this house, and he gave their description. They told him no. Then, in spite of my supplications, he insisted on going to the convent to inquire about them."

"What imprudence!" cried Adrienne.

"After what took place the other night, when he broke in," added Rodin, shrugging his shoulders.

"It was in vain to tell him," returned Mother Bunch, "that the letter did not announce positively, that the orphans would be delivered up to him; but that, no doubt, he would gain some information about them. He refused to hear anything, but said to me: 'If I cannot find them, I will rejoin you. But they were at the convent the day before yesterday, and now that all is discovered, they cannot refuse to give them up—"

"And with such a man there is no disputing!" said Rodin, with a smile.

"I hope they will not recognize him!" said Adrienne, remembering Baleinier's threats.

"It is not likely," replied Rodin; "they will only refuse him admittance. That will be, I hope, the worst misfortune that will happen. Besides, the magistrate will soon be here with the girls. I am no longer wanted: other cares require my attention. I must seek out Prince Djalma. Only tell me, my dear young lady, where I shall find you, to keep you informed of my discoveries, and to take measures with regard to the young prince, if my inquiries, as I hope, shall be attended with success."

"You will find me in my new house, Rue d'Anjou, formerly Beaulieu House. But now I think of it," said Adrienne, suddenly, after some moments of reflection, "it would not be prudent or proper, on many accounts, to lodge the Prince Djalma in the pavilion I occupied at Saint-Dizier House. I saw, some time ago, a charming little house, all furnished and ready; it only requires some embellishments, that could be completed in twenty four hours, to make it a delightful residence. Yes, that will be a thousand times preferable," added Mdlle. de Cardoville, after a new interval of silence; "and I shall thus be able to preserve the strictest incognito."

"What!" cried Rodin, whose projects would be much impeded by this new resolution of the young lady; "you do not wish him to know who you are?"

"I wish Prince Djalma to know absolutely nothing of the anonymous friend who comes to his aid; I desire that my name should not be pronounced before him, and that he should not even know of my existence—at least, for the present. Hereafter—in a month, perhaps—I will see; circumstances will guide me."

"But this incognito," said Rodin, hiding his disappointment, "will be difficult to preserve."

"If the prince had inhabited the lodge, I agree with you; the neighborhood of my aunt would have enlightened him, and this fear is one of the reasons that have induced me to renounce my first project. But the prince will inhabit a distant quarter—the Rue Blanche. Who will inform him of my secret? One of my old friends, M. Norval—you, sir—and this dear girl," pointing to Mother Bunch, "on whose discretion I can depend as on your own, will be my only confidants. My secret will then be quite safe. Besides, we will talk further on this subject to-morrow. You must begin by discovering the retreat of this unfortunate young prince."

Rodin, though much vexed at Adrienne's subtle determination with regard to Djalma, put the best face on the matter, and replied: "Your intentions shall be scrupulously fulfilled, my dear young lady; and to-morrow, with your leave, I hope to give you a good account of what you are pleased to call my providential mission."

"To-morrow, then, I shall expect you with impatience," said Adrienne, to Rodin, affectionately. "Permit me always to rely upon you, as from this day you may count upon me. You must be indulgent with me, sir; for I see that I shall yet have many counsels, many services to ask of you—though I already owe you so much."

"You will never owe me enough, my dear young lady, never enough," said Rodin, as he moved discreetly towards the door, after bowing to Adrienne. At the very moment he was going out, he found himself face to face with Dagobert.

"Holloa! at last I have caught one!" shouted the soldier, as he seized the Jesuit by the collar with a vigorous hand.

CHAPTER XXXVII.

EXCUSES.

On seeing Dagobert grasp Rodin so roughly by the collar, Mdlle. de Cardoville exclaimed in terror, as she advanced several steps towards the soldier: "In the name of Heaven, sir! what are you doing?"

"What am I doing?" echoed the soldier, harshly, without relaxing his hold on Rodin, and turning his head towards Adrienne, whom he did not know; "I take this opportunity to squeeze the throat of one of the wretches in the band of that renegade, until he tells me where my poor children are."

"You strangle me," said the Jesuit, in a stifled voice, as he tried to escape from the soldier.

"Where are the orphans, since they are not here, and the convent door has been closed against me?" cried Dagobert, in a voice of thunder.

"Help! help!" gasped Rodin.

"Oh! it is dreadful!" said Adrienne, as, pale and trembling, she held up her clasped hands to Dagobert. "Have mercy, sir! listen to me! listen to him!"

"M. Dagobert!" cried Mother Bunch, seizing with her weak hands the soldier's arm, and showing him Adrienne, "this is Mdlle. de Cardoville. What violence in her presence! and then, you are deceived doubtless!"

At the name of Mdlle. de Cardoville, the benefactress of his son, the soldier turned round suddenly, and loosened his hold on Rodin. The latter, crimson with rage and suffocation, set about adjusting his collar and his cravat.

"I beg your pardon, madame," said Dagobert, going towards Adrienne, who was still pale with fright; "I did not known who you were, and the first impulse of anger quite carried me away."

"But what has this gentleman done to you?" said Adrienne. "If you had listened to me, you would have learned—"

"Excuse me if I interrupt you, madame," said the soldier to Adrienne, in a hollow voice. Then addressing himself to Rodin, who had recovered his coolness, he added: "Thank the lady, and begone!—If you remain here, I will not answer for myself."

"One word only, my dear sir," said Rodin.

"I tell you that if you remain, I will not answer for myself!" cried Dagobert, stamping his foot.

"But, for heaven's sake, tell me the cause of this anger," resumed Adrienne; "above all, do not trust to appearances. Calm yourself, and listen."

"Calm myself, madame!" cried Dagobert, in despair; "I can think only of one thing, ma dame—of the arrival of Marshal Simon—he will be in Paris to-day or to-morrow."

"Is it possible?" said Adrienne. Rodin started with surprise and joy.

"Yesterday evening," proceeded Dagobert, "I received a letter from the marshal: he has landed at Havre. For three days I have taken step after step, hoping that the orphans would be restored to me, as the machinations of those wretches have failed." He pointed to Rodin with a new gesture of impatience. "Well! it is not so. They are conspiring some new infamy. I am prepared for anything."

"But, sir," said Rodin advancing, "permit me—"

"Begone!" cried Dagobert, whose irritation and anxiety redoubled, as he thought how at any moment Marshal Simon might arrive in Paris. "Begone! Were it not for this lady, I would at least be revenged on some one."

Rodin made a nod of intelligence to Adrienne, whom he approached prudently, and, pointing to Dagobert with a gesture of affectionate commiseration, he said to the latter: "I will leave you, sir, and the more willingly, as I was about to withdraw when you entered." Then, coming still closer to Mdlle. de Cardoville, the Jesuit whispered to her, "Poor soldier! he is beside himself with grief, and would be incapable of hearing me. Explain it all to him, my dear young lady; he will be nicely caught," added he, with a cunning air. "But in the meantime," resumed Rodin, feeling in the side-pocket of his great-coat and taking out a small parcel, "let me beg you to give him this, my dear young lady. It is my revenge, and a very good one."

And while Adrienne, holding the little parcel in her hand looked at the Jesuit with astonishment, the latter laying his forefinger upon his lip, as if recommending silence, drew backward on tiptoe to the door, and went out after again pointing to Dagobert with a gesture of pity; while the soldier, in sullen dejection, with his head drooping, and his arms crossed upon his bosom, remained deaf to the sewing-girl's earnest consolations. When Rodin had left the room, Adrienne, approaching the soldier, said to him, in her mild voice, with an expression of deep interest, "Your sudden entry prevented my asking you a question that greatly concerns me. How is your wound?"

"Thank you, madame," said Dagobert, starting from his painful lethargy, "it is of no consequence, but I have not time to think of it. I am sorry to have been so rough in your presence, and to have driven away that wretch; but 'tis more than I could master. At sight of those people, my blood is all up."

"And yet, believe me, you have been too hasty in your judgment. The person who was just now here—"

"Too hasty, madame! I do not see him to-day for the first time. He was with that renegade the Abbe d'Aigrigny—"

"No doubt!—and yet he is an honest and excellent man."

"He!" cried Dagobert.

"Yes; for at this moment he is busy about only one thing restoring to you those dear children!"

"He!" repeated Dagobert, as if he could not believe what he heard. "He restore me my children?"

"Yes; and sooner, perhaps, than you think for."

"Madame," said Dagobert, abruptly, "he deceives you. You are the dupe of that old rascal."

"No," said Adrienne, shaking her head, with a smile. "I have proofs of his good faith. First of all, it is he who delivers me from this house."

"Is it true?" said Dagobert, quite confounded.

"Very true; and here is, perhaps, something that will reconcile you to him," said Adrienne, as she delivered the small parcel which Rodin had given her as he went out. "Not wishing to exasperate you by his presence, he said to me: 'Give this to that brave soldier; it is my revenge.'"

Dagobert looked at Mdlle. de Cardoville with surprise, as he mechanically opened the little parcel. When he had unfolded it, and discovered his own silver cross, black with age, and the old red, faded ribbon, treasures taken from him at the White Falcon Inn, at the same time as his papers, he exclaimed in a broken voice: "My cross! my cross! It is my cross!" In the excitement of his joy, he pressed the silver star to his gray moustache.

Adrienne and the other were deeply affected by the emotion of the old soldier, who continued, as he ran towards the door by which Rodin had gone out: "Next to a service rendered to Marshal Simon, my wife, or son, nothing could be more precious to me. And you answer for this worthy man, madame, and I have ill used him in your presence! Oh! he is entitled to reparation, and he shall have it."

So saying, Dagobert left the room precipitately, hastened through two other apartments, gained the staircase, and descending it rapidly, overtook Rodin on the lowest step.

"Sir," said the soldier to him, in an agitated voice, as he seized him by the arm, "you must come upstairs directly."

"You should make up your mind to one thing or the other, my dear sir," said Rodin, stopping good-naturedly; "one moment you tell me to begone, and the next to return. How are we to decide?"

"Just now, sir, I was wrong; and when I am wrong, I acknowledge it. I abused and ill-treated you before witnesses; I will make you my apologies before witnesses."

"But, my dear sir—I am much obliged to you—I am in a hurry."

"I cannot help your being in a hurry. I tell you, I must have you come upstairs, directly—or else—or else," resumed Dagobert, taking the hand of the Jesuit, and pressing it with as much cordiality as emotion, "or else the happiness you have caused the in returning my cross will not be complete."

"Well, then, my good friend, let us go up."

"And not only have you restored me my cross, for which I have wept many tears, believe me, unknown to any one," cried Dagobert, much affected; "but the young lady told me, that, thanks to you, those poor children but tell me—no false joy-is it really true?—My God! is it really true?"

"Ah! ah! Mr. Inquisitive," said Rodin, with a cunning smile. Then he added: "Be perfectly tranquil, my growler; you shall have your two angels back again." And the Jesuit began to ascend the stairs.

"Will they be restored to me to-day?" cried Dagobert, stopping Rodin abruptly, by catching hold of his sleeve.

"Now, really, my good friend," said the Jesuit, "let us come to the point. Are we to go up or down? I do not find fault, but you turn me about like a teetotum."

"You are right. We shall be better able to explain things upstairs. Come with me—quick! quick!" said Dagobert, as, taking the Jesuit by the arm, he hurried him along, and brought him triumphantly into the room, where Adrienne and Mother Bunch had remained in much surprise at the soldier's sudden disappearance.

"Here he is! here he is!" cried Dagobert, as he entered. "Luckily, I caught him at the bottom of the stairs."

"And you have made me come up at a fine pace!" added Rodin, pretty well out of breath.

"Now, sir," said Dagobert, in a grave voice, "I declare, in presence of all, that I was wrong to abuse and ill-treat you. I make you my apology for it, sir; and I acknowledge, with joy, that I owe you—much—oh! very much and when I owe, I pay."

So saying, Dagobert held out his honest hand to Rodin, who pressed it in a very affable manner, and replied: "Now, really—what is all this about? What great service do you speak of?"

"This!" said Dagobert, holding up the cross before Rodin's eyes. "You do not know, then, what this cross is to me?"

"On the contrary, supposing you would set great store by it, I intended to have the pleasure of delivering it myself. I had brought it for that purpose; but, between ourselves, you gave me so warm a reception, that I had not the time—"

"Sir," said Dagobert, in confusion, "I assure you that I sincerely repent of what I have done."

"I know it, my good friend; do not say another word about it. You were then much attached to this cross?"

"Attached to it, sir!" cried Dagobert. "Why, this cross," and he kissed it as he spoke, "is my relic. He from whom it came was my saint—my hero—and he had touched it with his hand!"

"Oh!" said Rodin, feigning to regard the cross with as much curiosity as respectful admiration; "did Napoleon—the Great Napoleon—indeed touch with his own hand—that victorious hand!—this noble star of honor?"

"Yes, sir, with his own hand. He placed it there upon my bleeding breast, as a cure for my fifth wound. So that, you see, were I dying of hunger, I think I should not hesitate betwixt bread and my cross—that I might, in any case, have it on my heart in death. But, enough—enough! let us talk of something else. It is foolish in an old soldier, is it not?" added Dagobert, drawing his hand across his eyes, and then, as if ashamed to deny what he really felt: "Well, then! yes," he resumed, raising his head proudly, and no longer seeking to conceal the tears that rolled down his cheek; "yes, I weep for joy, to have found my cross—my cross, that the Emperor gave me with his victorious hand, as this worthy man has called it."

"Then blessed be my poor old hand for having restored you the glorious treasure!" said Rodin, with emotion. "In truth," he added, "the day will be a good one for everybody—as I announced to you this morning in my letter."

"That letter without a signature?" asked the soldier, more and more astonished. "Was it from you?"

"It was I who wrote it. Only, fearing some new snare of the Abbe d'Aigrigny, I did not choose, you understand, to explain myself more clearly."

"Then—I shall see—my orphans?"

Rodin nodded affirmatively, with an expression of great good-nature.

"Presently—perhaps immediately," said Adrienne, with smile. "Well! was I right in telling you that you had not judged this gentleman fairly?"

"Why did he not tell me this when I came in?" cried Dagobert, almost beside himself with joy.

"There was one difficulty in the way, my good friend," said Rodin; "it was, that when you came in, you nearly throttled me."

"True; I was too hasty. Once more, I ask your pardon. But was I to blame? I had only seen you with that Abbe d'Aigrigny, and in the first moment—"

"This dear young lady," said Rodin, bowing to Adrienne, "will tell you that I have been, without knowing it, the accomplice IN many perfidious actions; but as soon as I began to see my way through the darkness, I quitted the evil course on which I had entered, and returned to that which is honest, just and true."

Adrienne nodded affirmatively to Dagobert, who appeared to consult her look.

"If I did not sign the letter that I wrote to you, my good friend, it was partly from fear that my name might inspire suspicion; and if I asked you to come hither, instead of to the convent, it was that I had some dread—like this dear young lady—lest you might be recognized by the porter or by the gardener, your affair of the other night rendering such a recognition somewhat dangerous."

"But M. Baleinier knows all; I forgot that," said Adrienne, with uneasiness. "He threatened to denounce M. Dagobert and his son, if I made any complaint."

"Do not be alarmed, my dear young lady; it will soon be for you to dictate conditions," replied Rodin. "Leave that to me; and as for you, my good friend, your torments are now finished."

"Yes," said Adrienne, "an upright and worthy magistrate has gone to the convent, to fetch Marshal Simon's daughters. He will bring them hither; but he thought with me, that it would be most proper for them to take up their abode in my house. I cannot, however, come to this decision without your consent, for it is to you that these orphans were entrusted by their mother."

"You wish to take her place with regard to them, madame?" replied Dagobert. "I can only thank you with all my heart, for myself and for the children. But, as the lesson has been a sharp one, I must beg to remain at the door of their chamber, night and day. If they go out with you, I must be allowed to follow them at a little distance, so as to keep them in view, just like Spoil-sport, who has proved himself a better guardian than myself. When the marshal is once here—it will be in a day or two—my post will be relieved. Heaven grant it may be soon!"

"Yes," replied Rodin, in a firm voice, "heaven grant he may arrive soon, for he will have to demand a terrible reckoning of the Abbe d'Aigrigny, for the persecution of his daughters; and yet the marshal does not know all."

"And don't you tremble for the renegade?" asked Dagobert, as he thought how the marquis would soon find himself face to face with the marshal.

"I never care for cowards and traitors," answered Rodin; "and when Marshal Simon returns—" Then, after a pause of some seconds, he continued: "If he will do me the honor to hear me, he shall be edified as to the conduct of the Abbe d'Aigrigny. The marshal knows that his dearest friends, as well as himself, have been victims of the hatred of that dangerous man."

"How so?" said Dagobert.

"Why, yourself, for instance," replied Rodin; "you are an example of what I advance."

"Do you think it was mere chance, that brought about the scene at the White Falcon Inn, near Leipsic?"

"Who told you of that scene?" said Dagobert in astonishment.

"Where you accepted the challenge of Morok," continued the Jesuit, without answering Dagobert's question, "and so fell into a trap, or else refused it, and were then arrested for want of papers, and thrown into prison as a vagabond, with these poor children. Now, do you know the object of this violence? It was to prevent your being here on the 13th of February."

"But the more I hear, sir," said Adrienne, "the more I am alarmed at the audacity of the Abbe d'Aigrigny, and the extent of the means he has at his command. Really," she resumed, with increasing surprise, "if your words were not entitled to absolute belief—"

"You would doubt their truth, madame?" said Dagobert. "It is like me. Bad as he is. I cannot think that this renegade had relations with a wild-beast showman as far off as Saxony; and then, how could he know that I and the children were to pass through Leipsic? It is impossible, my good man."

"In fact, sir," resumed Adrienne, "I fear that you are deceived by your dislike (a very legitimate one) of Abbe d'Aigrigny, and that you ascribe to him an almost fabulous degree of power and extent of influence."

After a moment's silence, during which Rodin looked first at Adrienne and then at Dagobert, with a kind of pity, he resumed. "How could the Abbe d'Aigrigny have your cross in his possession, if he had no connection with Morok?"

"That is true, sir," said Dagobert; "joy prevented me from reflecting. But how indeed, did my cross come into your hands?"

"By means of the Abbe d'Aigrigny's having precisely those relations with Leipsic, of which you and the young lady seem to doubt."

"But how did my cross get to Paris?"

"Tell me; you were arrested at Leipsic for want of papers—is it not so?"

"Yes; but I could never understand how my passports and money disappeared from my knapsack. I thought I must have had the misfortune to lose them."

Rodin shrugged his shoulders, and replied: "You were robbed of them at the White Falcon Inn, by Goliath, one of Morok's servants, and the latter sent the papers and the cross to the Abbe d'Aigrigny, to prove that he had succeeded in executing his orders with respect to the orphans and yourself. It was the day before yesterday, that I obtained the key of that dark machination. Cross and papers were amongst the stores of Abbe d'Aigrigny; the papers formed a considerable bundle, and he might have missed them; but, hoping to see you this morning, and knowing how a soldier of the Empire values his cross, his sacred relic, as you call it, my good friend—I did not hesitate. I put the relic into my pocket. 'After all,' said I, 'it is only restitution, and my delicacy perhaps exaggerates this breach of trust.'"

"You could not have done a better action," said Adrienne; "and, for my part, because of the interest I feel for M. Dagobert—I take it as a personal favor. But, sir," after a moment's silence, she resumed with anxiety: "What terrible power must be at the command of M. d'Aigrigny, for him to have such extensive and formidable relations in a foreign country!"

"Silence!" said Rodin, in a low voice, and looking round him with an air of alarm. "Silence! In heaven's name do not ask me about it!"

CHAPTER XXXVIII.

REVELATIONS.

Mdlle. de Cardoville, much astonished at the alarm displayed by Rodin, when she had asked him for some explanation of the formidable and far reaching power of the Abby d'Aigrigny, said to him: "Why, sir, what is there so strange in the question that I have just asked you?"

After a moment's silence, Rodin cast his looks all around, with well feigned uneasiness, and replied in a whisper: "Once more, madame, do not question me on so fearful a subject. The walls of this house may have ears."

Adrienne and Dagobert looked at each other with growing surprise. Mother Bunch, by an instinct of incredible force, continued to regard Rodin with invincible suspicion. Sometimes she stole a glance at him, as if trying to penetrate the mask of this man, who filled her with fear. At one moment, the Jesuit encountered her anxious gaze, obstinately fixed upon him; immediately he nodded to her with the greatest amenity. The young girl, alarmed at finding herself observed, turned away with a shudder.

"No, no, my dear young lady," resumed Rodin, with a sigh, as he saw Mdlle. de Cardoville astonished at his silence; "do not question me on the subject of the Abbe d'Aigrigny's power!"

"But, to persist, sir," said Adrienne; "why this hesitation to answer? What do you fear?"

"Ah, my dear young lady," said Rodin, shuddering, "those people are so powerful! their animosity is so terrible!"

"Be satisfied, sir; I owe you too much, for my support ever to fail you."

"Ah, my dear young lady," cried Rodin, as if hurt by the supposition; "think better of me, I entreat you. Is it for myself that I fear?—No, no; I am too obscure, too inoffensive; but it is for you, for Marshal Simon, for the other members of your family, that all is to be feared. Oh, my dear young lady! let me beg you to ask no questions. There are secrets which are fatal to those who possess them."

"But, sir, is it not better to know the perils with which one is threatened?"

"When you know the manoeuvres of your enemy, you may at least defend yourself," said Dagobert. "I prefer an attack in broad daylight to an ambuscade."

"And I assure you," resumed Adrienne, "the few words you have spoken cause me a vague uneasiness."

"Well, if I must, my dear young lady," replied the Jesuit, appearing to make a great effort, "since you do not understand my hints, I will be more explicit; but remember," added he, in a deeply serious tone, "that you have persevered in forcing me to tell you what you had perhaps better not have known."

"Speak, Sir, I pray you speak," said Adrienne.

Drawing about him Adrienne, Dagobert, and Mother Bunch, Rodin said to them in a low voce, and with a mysterious air: "Have you never heard of a powerful association, which extends its net over all the earth, and counts its disciples, agents, and fanatics in every class of society which has had, and often has still, the ear of kings and nobles—which, in a word, can raise its creatures to the highest positions, and with a word can reduce them again to the nothingness from which it alone could uplift them?"

"Good heaven, sir!" said Adrienne, "what formidable association? Until now I never heard of it."

"I believe you; and yet your ignorance on this subject greatly astonishes me, my dear young lady."

"And why should it astonish you?"

"Because you lived some time with your aunt, and must have often seen the Abbe d'Aigrigny."

"I lived at the princess's, but not with her; for a thousand reasons she had inspired me with warrantable aversion."

"In truth, my dear young lady, my remark was ill-judged. It was there, above all, and particularly in your presence, that they would keep silence with regard to this association—and yet to it alone did the Princess de Saint-Dizier owe her formidable influence in the world, during the last reign. Well, then; know this—it is the aid of that association which renders the Abbe d'Aigrigny so dangerous a man.

"By it he was enabled to follow and to reach divers members of your family, some in Siberia, some in India, others on the heights of the American mountains; but, as I have told you, it was only the day before yesterday, and by chance, that, examining the papers of Abbe d'Aigrigny, I found the trace of his connection with this Company, of which he is the most active and able chief."

"But the name, sir, the name of this Company?" said Adrienne.

"Well! it is—" but Rodin stopped short.

"It is," repeated Adrienne, who was now as much interested as Dagobert and the sempstress; "it is—"

Rodin looked round him, beckoned all the actors in this scene to draw nearer, and said in a whisper, laying great stress upon the words: "It is—the Society of Jesus!" and he again shuddered.

"The Jesuits!" cried Mdlle. de Cardoville, unable to restrain a burst of laughter, which was the more buoyant, as, from the mysterious precautions of Rodin, she had expected some very different revelation. "The Jesuits!" she resumed, still laughing. "They have no existence, except in books; they are frightful historical personages, certainly; but why should you put forward Madame de Saint-Dizier and M. d'Aigrigny in that character? Such as they are, they have done quite enough to justify my aversion and disdain."

After listening in silence to Mdlle. de Cardoville Rodin continued, with a grave and agitated air: "Your blindness frightens me, my dear, young lady; the past should have given you some anxiety for the future, since, more than any one, you have already suffered from the fatal influence of this Company, whose existence you regard as a dream!"

"I, sir?" said Adrienne, with a smile, although a little surprised.

"You."

"Under what circumstances?"

"You ask me this question! my dear young lady! you ask me this question!—and yet you have been confined here as a mad person! Is it not enough to tell you that the master of this house is one of the most devoted lay members of the Company, and therefore the blind instrument of the Abbe d'Aigrigny?"

"So," said Adrienne, this time without smiling, "Dr. Baleinier"

"Obeyed the Abbe d'Aigrigny, the most formidable chief of that formidable society. He employs his genius for evil; but I must confess he is a man of genius. Therefore, it is upon him that you and yours must fix all your doubts and suspicions; it is against him that you must be upon your guard. For, believe me, I know him, and he does not look upon the game as lost. You must be prepared for new attacks, doubtless of another kind, but only the more dangerous on that account—"

"Luckily, you give us notice," said Dagobert, "and you will be on our side."

"I can do very little, my good friends; but that little is at the service of honest people," said Rodin.

"Now," said Adrienne, with a thoughtful air, completely persuaded by Rodin's air of conviction, "I can explain the inconceivable influence that my aunt exercised in the world. I ascribed it chiefly to her relations with persons in power; I thought that she, like the Abbe d'Aigrigny, was concerned in dark intrigues, for which religion served as a veil—but I was far from believing what you tell me."

"How many things you have got to learn!" resumed Rodin. "If you knew, my dear young lady, with what art these people surround you, without your being aware of it, by agents devoted to themselves! Every one of your steps is known to them, when they have any interest in such knowledge. Thus, little by little, they act upon you—slowly, cautiously, darkly. They circumvent you by every possible means, from flattery to terror—seduce or frighten, in order at last to rule you, without your being conscious of their authority. Such is their object, and I must confess they pursue it with detestable ability."

Rodin had spoken with so much sincerity, that Adrienne trembled; then, reproaching herself with these fears, she resumed: "And yet, no—I can never believe in so infernal a power; the might of priestly ambition belongs to another age. Heaven be praised, it has disappeared forever!"

"Yes, certainly, it is out of sight; for they now know how to disperse and disappear, when circumstances require it. But then are they the most dangerous; for suspicion is laid asleep, and they keep watch in the dark. Oh! my dear young lady, if you knew their frightful ability! In my hatred of all that is oppressive, cowardly, and hypocritical, I had studied the history of that terrible society, before I knew that the Abbe d'Aigrigny belonged to it. Oh! it is dreadful. If you knew what means they employ! When I tell you that, thanks to their diabolical devices, the most pure and devoted appearances often conceal the most horrible snares." Rodin's eye rested, as if by chance, on the hunchback; but, seeing that Adrienne did not take the hint, the Jesuit continued: "In a word—are you not exposed to their pursuits?—have they any interest in gaining you over?—oh! from that moment, suspect all that surround you, suspect the most noble attachments, the most tender affections, for these monsters sometimes succeed in corrupting your best friends, and making a terrible use of them, in proportion to the blindness of your confidence."

"Oh! it is impossible," cried Adrienne, in horror. "You must exaggerate. No! hell itself never dreamed of more frightful treachery!"

"Alas, my dear young lady! one of your relations, M. Hardy—the most loyal and generous-hearted man that could be—has been the victim of some such infamous treachery. Do you know what we learned from the reading of your ancestor's will? Why, that he died the victim of the malevolence of these people; and now, at the lapse of a hundred and fifty years, his descendants are still exposed to the hate of that indestructible society."

"Oh, sir! it terrifies me," said Adrienne, feeling her heart sink within her. "But are there no weapons against such attacks?"

"Prudence, my dear young lady—the most watchful caution—the most incessant study and suspicion of all that approach you."

"But such a life would be frightful! It is a torture to be the victim of continual suspicions, doubts, and fears."

"Without doubt! They know it well, the wretches! That constitutes their strength. They often triumph by the very excess of the precautions taken against them. Thus, my dear young lady, and you, brave and worthy soldier, in the name of all that is dear to you, be on your guard, and do not lightly impart your confidence. Be on your guard, for you have nearly fallen the victims of those people. They will always be your implacable enemies. And you, also, poor, interesting girl!" added the Jesuit, speaking to Mother Bunch, "follow my advice—fear these people. Sleep, as the proverb says, with one eye open."

"I, sir!" said the work-girl. "What have I done? what have I to fear?"

"What have you done? Dear me! Do not you tenderly love this young lady, your protectress? have you not attempted to assist her? Are you not the adopted sister of the son of this intrepid soldier, the brave Agricola! Alas, poor, girl! are not these sufficient claims to their hatred, in spite of your obscurity? Nay, my dear young lady! do not think that I exaggerate. Reflect! only reflect! Think what I have just said to the faithful companion-in-arms of Marshal Simon, with regard to his imprisonment at Leipsic. Think what happened to yourself, when, against all law and reason, you were brought hither. Then you will see, that there is nothing exaggerated in the picture I have drawn of the secret power of this Company. Be always on your guard, and, in doubtful cases, do not fear to apply to me. In three days, I have learned enough by my own experience, with regard to their manner of acting, to be able to point out to you many a snare, device, and danger, and to protect you from them."

"In any such case, sir," replied Mdlle. de Cardoville, "my interests, as well as gratitude, would point to you as my best counsellor."

According to the skillful tactics of the sons of Loyola, who sometimes deny their own existence, in order to escape from an adversary—and sometimes proclaim with audacity the living power of their organization, in order to intimidate the feeble-R-odin had laughed in the face of the bailiff of Cardoville, when the latter had spoken of the existence of the Jesuits; while now, at this moment, picturing their means of action, he endeavored, and he succeeded in the endeavor, to impregnate the mind of Mdlle. de Cardoville with some germs of doubt, which were gradually to develop themselves by reflection, and serve hereafter the dark projects that he meditated. Mother Bunch still felt considerable alarm with regard to Rodin. Yet, since she had heard the fatal powers of the formidable Order revealed to Adrienne, the young sempstress, far from suspecting the Jesuit of having the audacity to speak thus of a society of which he was himself a member, felt grateful to him, in spite of herself, for the important advice that he had just given her patroness. The side-glance which she now cast upon him (which Rodin also detected, for he watched the young girl with sustained attention), was full of gratitude, mingled with surprise. Guessing the nature of this impression, and wishing entirely to remove her unfavorable opinion, and also to anticipate a revelation which would be made sooner or later, the Jesuit appeared to have forgotten something of great importance, and exclaimed, striking his forehead: "What was I thinking of?" Then, speaking to Mother Bunch, he added: "Do you know where your sister is, my dear girl?" Disconcerted and saddened by this unexpected question, the workwoman answered with a blush, for she remembered her last interview with the brilliant Bacchanal Queen: "I have not seen my sister for some days, sir."

"Well, my dear girl, she is not very comfortable," said Rodin; "I promised one of her friends to send her some little assistance. I have applied to a charitable person, and that is what I received for her." So saying, he drew from his pocket a sealed roll of coin, which he delivered to Mother Bunch, who was now both surprised and affected.

"You have a sister in trouble, and I know nothing of it?" said Adrienne, hastily. "This is not right of you, my child!"

"Do not blame her," said Rodin. "First of all, she did not know that her sister was in distress, and, secondly, she could not ask you, my dear young lady, to interest yourself about her."

As Mdlle. de Cardoville looked at Rodin with astonishment, he added, again speaking to the hunchback: "Is not that true, my dear girl!"

"Yes, sir," said the sempstress, casting down her eyes and blushing. Then she added, hastily and anxiously: "But when did you see my sister, sir? where is she? how did she fall into distress?"

"All that would take too long to tell you, my dear girl; but go as soon as possible to the greengrocer's in the Rue Clovis, and ask to speak to your sister as from M. Charlemagne or M. Rodin, which you please, for I am equally well known in that house by my Christian name as by my surname, and then you will learn all about it. Only tell your sister, that, if she behaves well, and keeps to her good resolutions, there are some who will continue to look after her."

More and more surprised, Mother Bunch was about to answer Rodin, when the door opened, and M. de Gernande entered. The countenance of the magistrate was grave and sad.

"Marshal Simon's daughters!" cried Mdlle. de Cardoville.

"Unfortunately, they are not with me," answered the judge.

"Then, where are they, sir? What have they done with them? The day before yesterday, they were in the convent!" cried Dagobert, overwhelmed by this complete destruction of his hopes.

Hardly had the soldier pronounced these words, when, profiting by the impulse which gathered all the actors in this scene about the magistrate, Rodin withdrew discreetly towards the door, and disappeared without any one perceiving his absence. Whilst the soldier, thus suddenly thrown back to the depths of his despair, looked at M. de Gernande, waiting with anxiety for the answer, Adrienne said to the magistrate: "But, sir, when you applied at the convent, what explanation did the superior give on the subject of these young girls?"

"The lady superior refused to give any explanation, madame. 'You pretend,' said she, 'that the young persons of whom you speak are detained here against their will. Since the law gives you the right of entering this house, make your search.' 'But, madame, please to answer me positively,' said I to the superior; 'do you declare, that you know nothing of the young girls, whom I have come to claim?' 'I have nothing to say on this subject, sir. You assert, that you are authorized to make a search: make it.' Not being able to get any other explanation," continued the magistrate, "I searched all parts of the convent, and had every door opened—but, unfortunately, I could find no trace of these young ladies."

"They must have sent them elsewhere," cried Dagobert; "who knows?—perhaps, ill. They will kill them—O God! they will kill them!" cried he, in a heart-rending tone.

"After such a refusal, what is to be done? Pray, sir, give us your advice; you are our providence," said Adrienne, turning to speak to Rodin, who she fancied was behind her. "What is your—"

Then, perceiving that the Jesuit had suddenly disappeared, she said to Mother Bunch, with uneasiness: "Where is M. Rodin?"

"I do not know, madame," answered the girl, looking round her; "he is no longer here."

"It is strange," said Adrienne, "to disappear so abruptly!"

"I told you he was a traitor!" cried Dagobert, stamping with rage; "they are all in a plot together."

"No, no," said Mdlle. de Cardoville; "do not think that. But the absence is not the less to be regretted, for, under these difficult circumstances, he might have given us very useful information, thanks to the position he occupied at M. d'Aigrigny's."

"I confess, madame, that I rather reckoned upon it," said M. de Gernande; "and I returned hither, not only to inform you of the fruitless result of my search, but also to seek from the upright and honorable roan, who so courageously unveiled these odious machinations, the aid of his counsels in this contingency."

Strangely enough, for the last few moments Dagobert was so completely absorbed in thought, that he paid no attention to the words of the magistrate, however important to him. He did not even perceive the departure of M. de Gernande, who retired after promising Adrienne that he would neglect no means to arrive at the truth, in regard to the disappearance of the orphans. Uneasy at this silence, wishing to quit the house immediately, and induce Dagobert to accompany her, Adrienne, after exchanging a rapid glance with Mother Bunch, was advancing towards the soldier, when hasty steps were heard from without the chamber, and a manly sonorous voice, exclaiming with impatience, "Where is he—where is he?"

At the sound of this voice, Dagobert seemed to rouse himself with a start, made a sudden bound, and with a loud cry, rushed towards the door. It opened. Marshal Simon appeared on the threshold!

CHAPTER XXXIX.

PIERRE SIMON.

Marshal Pierre Simon, Duke de Ligny, was a man of tall stature, plainly dressed in a blue frock-coat, buttoned up to the throat, with a red ribbon tied to the top buttonhole. You could not have wished to see a more frank, honest, and chivalrous cast of countenance than the marshal's. He had a broad forehead, an aquiline nose, a well formed chin, and a complexion bronzed by exposure to the Indian sun. His hair, cut very short, was inclined to gray about the temples; but his eyebrows were still as black as his large, hanging moustache. His walk was free and bold, and his decided movements showed his military impetuosity. A man of the people, a man of war and action, the frank cordiality of his address invited friendliness and sympathy. As enlightened as he was intrepid as generous as he was sincere, his manly, plebeian pride was the most remarkable part of his character. As others are proud of their high birth, so was he of his obscure origin, because it was ennobled by the fine qualities of his father, the rigid republican, the intelligent and laborious artisan, who, for the space of forty years, had been the example and the glory of his fellow-workmen. In accepting with gratitude the aristocratic title which the Emperor had bestowed upon him, Pierre Simon acted with that delicacy which receives from a friendly hand a perfectly useless gift, and estimates it according to the intention of the giver. The religious veneration of Pierre Simon for the Emperor had never been blind; in proportion as his devotion and love for his idol were instructive and necessary, his admiration was serious, and founded upon reason. Far from resembling those swashbucklers who love fighting for its own sake, Marshal Simon not only admired his hero as the greatest captain in the world, but he admired him, above all, because he knew that the Emperor had only accepted war in the hope of one day being able to dictate universal peace; for if peace obtained by glory and strength is great, fruitful, and magnificent, peace yielded by weakness and cowardice is sterile, disastrous, and dishonoring. The son of a workman, Pierre Simon still further admired the Emperor, because that imperial parvenu had always known how to make that popular heart beat nobly, and, remembering the people, from the masses of whom he first arose, had invited them fraternally to share in regal and aristocratic pomp.

When Marshal Simon entered the room, his countenance was much agitated. At sight of Dagobert, a flash of joy illumined his features; he rushed towards the soldier, extending his arms, and exclaimed, "My friend! my old friend!"

Dagobert answered this affectionate salute with silent emotion. Then the marshal, disengaging himself from his arms, and fixing his moist eyes upon him, said to him in so agitated a voice that his lips trembled, "Well, didst arrive in time for the 13th of February?"

"Yes, general; but everything is postponed for four months."

"And—my wife?—my child?" At this question Dagobert shuddered, hung down his head, and was silent.

"They are not, then, here?" asked Simon, with more surprise than uneasiness. "They told me they were not at your house, but that I should find you here—and I came immediately. Are they not with you?"

"General," said Dagobert, becoming deadly pale; "general—" Drying the drops of cold sweat that stood upon his forehead, he was unable to articulate a word, for his voice was checked in his parched throat.

"You frighten me!" exclaimed Pierre Simon, becoming pale as the soldier, and seizing him by the arm.

At this, Adrienne advanced, with a countenance full of grief and sympathy; seeing the cruel embarrassment of Dagobert, she wished to come to his assistance, and she said to Pierre Simon, in a mild but agitated voice, "Marshal, I am Mdlle. de Cardoville—a relation of your dear children."

Pierre Simon turned around suddenly, as much struck with the dazzling beauty of Adrienne as with the words she had just pronounced. He stammered out in his surprise, "You, madame—a relation—of my children!"

He laid a stress on the last words, and looked at Dagobert in a kind of stupor.

"Yes, marshal your children," hastily replied Adrienne; "and the love of those charming twin sisters—"

"Twin sisters!" cried Pierre Simon, interrupting Mdlle. de Cardoville, with an outburst of joy impossible to describe. "Two daughters instead of one! Oh! what happiness for their mother! Pardon me, madame, for being so impolite," he continued; "and so little grateful for what you tell me. But you will understand it; I have been seventeen years without seeing my wife; I come, and I find three loved beings, instead of two. Thanks, madame: would I could express all the gratitude I owe you! You are our relation; this is no doubt your house; my wife and children are with you. Is it so? You think that my sudden appearance might be prejudicial to them? I will wait—but madame, you, that I am certain are good as fair—pity my impatience—will make haste to prepare them to receive me—"

More and more agitated, Dagobert avoided the marshal's gaze, and trembled like a leaf. Adrienne cast down her eyes without answering. Her heart sunk within her, at thought of dealing the terrible blow to Marshal Simon.

The latter, astonished at this silence, looking at Adrienne, then at the soldier, became first uneasy, and at last alarmed. "Dagobert!" he exclaimed, "something is concealed from me!"

"General!" stammered the soldier, "I assure you—I—I—."

"Madame!" cried Pierre Simon, "I conjure you, in pity, speak to me frankly!—my anxiety is horrible. My first fears return upon me. What is it? Are my wife and daughters ill? Are they in danger? Oh! speak! speak!"

"Your daughters, marshal," said Adrienne "have been rather unwell, since their long journey—but they are in no danger."

"Oh, heaven! it is my wife!"

"Have courage, sir!" said Mdlle. de Cardoville, sadly. "Alas! you must seek consolation in the affection of the two angels that remain to you."

"General!" said Dagobert, in a firm grave tone, "I returned from Siberia—alone with your two daughters."

"And their mother! their mother!" cried Simon, in a voice of despair.

"I set out with the two orphans the day after her death," said the soldier.

"Dead?" exclaimed Pierre Simon, overwhelmed by the stroke; "dead?" A mournful silence was the only answer. The marshal staggered beneath this unexpected shock, leaned on the back of a chair for support, and then, sinking into the seat, concealed his face with his hands. For same minutes nothing was heard but stifled sobs, for not only had Pierre Simon idolized his wife, but by one of those singular compromises, that a man long cruelly tried sometimes makes with destiny, Pierre Simon, with the fatalism of loving souls, thought he had a right to reckon upon happiness after so many years of suffering, and had not for a moment doubted that he should find his wife and child—a double consolation reserved to him after going through so much. Very different from certain people, whom the habit of misfortune renders less exacting, Simon had reckoned upon happiness as complete as had been his misery. His wife and child were the sole, indispensable conditions of this felicity, and, had the mother survived her daughters, she would have no more replaced them in his eyes than they did her. Weakness or avarice of the heart, so it was; we insist upon this singularity, because the consequences of these incessant and painful regrets exercised a great influence on the future life of Marshal Simon. Adrienne and Dagobert had respected the overwhelming grief of this unfortunate man. When he had given a free course to his tears, he raised his manly countenance, now of marble paleness, drew his hand across his blood-shot eyes, rose, and said to Adrienne, "Pardon me, madame; I could not conquer my first emotion. Permit me to retire. I have cruel details to ask of the worthy friend who only quitted my wife at the last moment. Have the kindness to let me see my children—my poor orphans!—" And the marshal's voice again broke.

"Marshal," said Mdlle. de Cardoville, "just now we were expecting your dear children: unfortunately, we have been deceived in our hopes." Pierre Simon first looked at Adrienne without answering, as if he had not heard or understood.—"But console yourself," resumed the young girl; "we have yet no reason to despair."

"To despair?" repeated the marshaling by turns at Mdlle. de Cardoville despair?—"of what, in heaven's name?"

"Of seeing your children, marshal," said Adrienne; "the presence of their father will facilitate the search."

"The search!" cried Pierre Simon. "Then, my daughters are not here?"

"No, sir," said Adrienne, at length; "they have been taken from the affectionate care of the excellent man who brought them from Russia, to be removed to a convent."

"Wretch!" cried Pierre Simon, advancing towards Dagobert, with a menacing and terrible aspect; "you shall answer to me for all!"

"Oh, sir, do not blame him!" cried Mdlle. de Cardoville.

"General," said Dagobert, in a tone of mournful resignation, "I merit your anger. It is my fault. Forced to absent myself from Paris, I entrusted the children to my wife; her confessor turned her head, and persuaded her that your daughters would be better in a convent than at our house. She believed him, and let them be conveyed there. Now they say at the convent, that they do not know where they are. This is the truth: do what you will with me; I have only to silently endure."

"This is infamous!" cried Pierre Simon, pointing to Dagobert, with a gesture of despairing indignation. "In whom can a man confide, if he has deceived me? Oh, my God!"

"Stay, marshal! do not blame him," repeated Mdlle. de Cardoville; "do not think so! He has risked life and honor to rescue your children from the convent. He is not the only one who has failed in this attempt. Just now, a magistrate—despite his character and authority—was not more successful.

His firmness towards the superior, his minute search of the convent, were all in vain. Up to this time it has been impossible to find these unfortunate children."

"But where's this convent!" cried Marshal Simon, raising his head, his face all pale and agitated with grief and rage. "Where is it? Do these vermin know what a father is, deprived of his children?" At the moment when Marshal Simon, turning towards Dagobert, pronounced these words, Rodin, holding Rose and Blanche by the hand, appeared at the open door of the chamber. On hearing the marshal's exclamation, he started with surprise, and a flash of diabolical joy lit up his grim countenance—for he had not expected to meet Pierre Simon so opportunely.

Mdlle. de Cardoville was the first to perceive the presence of Rodin. She exclaimed, as she hastened towards him: "Oh! I was not deceived. He is still our providence."

"My poor children!" said Rodin, in a low voice, to the young girls, as he pointed to Pierre Simon, "this is your father!"

"Sir!" cried Adrienne, following close upon Rose and Blanche. "Your children are here!"

As Simon turned round abruptly, his two daughters threw themselves into his arms. Here was a long silence, broken only by sobs, and kisses, and exclamations of joy.

"Come forward, at least, and enjoy the good you have done!" said Mdlle. de Cardoville, drying her eyes, and turning towards Rodin, who, leaning against the door, seemed to contemplate this scene with deep emotion.

Dagobert, at sight of Rodin bringing back the children, was at first struck with stupor, and unable to move a step; but hearing the words of Adrienne, and yielding to a burst of almost insane gratitude, he threw himself on his knees before the Jesuit, joined his hands together, and exclaimed in a broken voice: "You have saved me, by bringing back these children."

"Oh, bless you, sir!" said Mother Bunch, yielding to the general current.

"My good friends, this is too much," said Rodin, as if his emotions were beyond his strength; "this is really too much for me. Excuse me to the marshal, and tell him that I am repaid by the sight of his happiness."

"Pray, sir," said Adrienne, "let the marshal at least have the opportunity to see and know you."

"Oh, remain! you that have saved us all!" cried Dagobert, trying to stop Rodin.

"Providence, you know, my dear young lady, does not trouble itself about the good that is done, but the good that remains to do," said Rodin, with an accent of playful kindness. "Must I not think of Prince Djalma? My task is not finished, and moments are precious. Come," he added, disengaging himself gently from Dagobert's hold, "come the day has been as good a one as I had hoped.. The Abbe d'Aigrigny is unmasked; you are free, my dear young lady; you have recovered your cross, my brave soldier; Mother Bunch is sure of a protectress; the marshal has found his children. I have my share in all these joys, it is a full share—my heart is satisfied. Adieu, my friends, till we meet again." So saying, Rodin waved his hand affectionately to Adrienne, Dagobert, and the hunchback, and withdrew, waving his hand with a look of delight on Marshal Simon, who, seated between his daughters, held them in his arms, and covered them with tears and kisses, remaining quite indifferent to all that was passing around him.

An hour after this scene, Mdlle. de Cardoville and the sempstress, Marshal Simon, his two daughters and Dagobert quitted Dr. Beleinier's asylum.

In terminating this episode, a few words by way of moral, with regard to lunatic asylums and convents may not be out of place. We have said, and we repeat, that the laws which apply to the superintendence of lunatic asylums appear to us insufficient. Facts that have recently transpired before the courts, and other facts that have been privately communicated to us, evidently prove this insufficiency. Doubtless, magistrates have full power to visit lunatic asylums. They are even required to make such visits. But we know, from the best authority, that the numerous and pressing occupations of magistrates, whose number is often out of proportion with the labor imposed upon them, render these inspections so rare, that they are, so to speak, illusory. It appears, therefore, to us advisable to institute a system of inspections, at least twice a month, especially designed for lunatic asylums, and entrusted to a physician and a magistrate, so that every complaint may be submitted to a double examination. Doubtless, the law is sufficient when its ministers are fully informed; but how many formalities, how many difficulties must be gone through, before they can be so, particularly when the unfortunate creature who needs their assistance, already suspected, isolated, and imprisoned, has no friend to come forward in defence, and demand, in his or her name, the protection of the authorities! Is it not imperative, therefore, on the civil power, to meet these necessities by a periodical and well-organized system of inspection?

What we here say of lunatic asylums will apply with still greater force to convents for women, seminaries, and houses inhabited by religious bodies. Recent and notorious facts, with which all France has rung, have, unfortunately, proved that violence, forcible detention, barbarous usage, abduction of minors, and illegal imprisonment, accompanied by torture, are occurrences which, if not frequent, are at least possible in religious houses. It required singular accidents, audacious and cynical brutalities; to bring these detestable actions to public knowledge. How many other victims have been, and, perhaps still are, entombed in those large silent mansions, where no profane look may penetrate, and which, through the privileges of the clergy, escape the superintendence of the civil power. Is it not deplorable that these dwellings should not also be subject to periodical inspection, by visitors consisting, if it be desired, of a priest, a magistrate, and some delegate of the municipal authorities? If nothing takes place, but what is legal, human, and charitable, in these establishments, which have all the character, and incur all the responsibility, of public institutions, why this resistance, this furious indignation of the church party, when any mention is made of touching what they call their privileges? There is something higher than the constitutions devised at Rome. We mean the Law of France—the common law—which grants to all protection, but which, in return, exacts from all respect and obedience.

www.ingramcontent.com/pod-product-compliance
Ingram Content Group UK Ltd.
Pitfield, Milton Keynes, MK11 3LW, UK
UKHW041019120225
455007UK00004B/217